Praise for *The Temp*

"What makes *The Temple of Air* such an immersive read depth McNair brings to a variety of characters, whether they are cynical teenagers or Bible-thumping adults."
— *TimeOut Chicago*

"These stories speak to us in voices that are clear, urgent, tough, and shockingly wise. McNair's *The Temple of Air* is about the spiritual resilience of endangered children, the survival methods of battered adults, and the presence of grace even in our ruined century."
— David Huddle, author of *The Story of a Million Years*

"The stories in *The Temple of Air* are steeped in a particular brand of hospitality and violence. They are definitively Midwestern, navigating deftly between the everyday and the disturbing, the prosaic and the poetic."
— *Newcity Chicago*

"The Temple of Air is a collection of fever-dreams: often haunting, always beautiful. These are lyrical stories that sear themselves into the reader's subconscious, and we are incredibly lucky to have them."
— John McNally, author of *After the Workshop*

"These narratives are fierce, fearless, brave, as stylistically pure as Ray Carver, as hard hitting as Mary Gaitskill, as lyrically impassioned as Stu Dybek. Still, McNair is an original, even when her characters miss their good chances or hurt what they love, we feel compassion, we hear the pure note of human pathos. You won't be able to put these stories down."

— Anne-Marie Oomen, author of *An American Map*

"The voices of McNair's characters whisper directly into your ear, inhabiting their stories so completely that the author herself becomes invisible, and the stories simply flow, looping gracefully backward and forward, encircling and encompassing one another like an ancient Celtic etching. *The Temple of Air* is a wise and masterful book."

— Dennis McFadden, author of *Hart's Grove*

Patricia Ann McNair selected as one of *Newcity*'s "Lit 50: Who Really Books in Chicago 2012."

THE TEMPLE OF *Air*

THE TEMPLE OF *Air*

STORIES

PATRICIA ANN McNAIR

ELEPHANT
ROCK
BOOKS

Published by
Elephant Rock Books
Bloomington, Indiana
www.erpmedia.net/books

First Edition
10 9 8 7 6 5 4

Library of Congress Control Number: 2011920047

ISBN: 0615434630

ISBN 13: 978-0-615-43463-6

Book Design: Melissa C. Lucar

Cover Photo: © Jeff Biglan (iStockphoto)

Printed in the United States of America

Dedicated to the memory of my mother,
Sylvia McNair

CONTENTS

THE TEMPLE OF

Air

SOMETHING LIKE FAITH

And even as it happened, Nova could not believe it. "Jim," the wife said, Nova heard her. Like "Jim, pass the salt," or something. But he turned then from where he stood in the center of the gondola, just a little shift, a slight release of all that attention he was giving his tiny, tiny girl—*whee*ing her like that, in and out, in and out, his arms a hammock, one two three *whee*. Nova'd been watching, scrunched in there between the boys, on their own side of the ride. She hadn't wanted to go anyway, she was fucked up and scared of heights and it was a stupid shit carnival ride: "The Gondolier," big swinging cages, all that air. "Don't," someone must have said, but then the dad turned that slight, small shift, away from that last out swing toward those ridiculous, wide-spaced bars that are somehow supposed to keep everyone safe, but clearly can't when the dad turns his head, his attention, just a bit away but enough so the little girl (a baby, really, all tiny and tickly, all screaming and squirming) tilts somehow and slips from Dad's arms, his hands. His fingers open up and his grip unfolds and gives way beneath the weight of her rolling off and apart from him and through the bars and over over over the side and down down down through the sky. And then it all runs together. The moments before and after become one absolutely single moment, a knot of time and activity that moves in a slow circle with the big carnival wheel. The dad goes down, just like that, sinks to his knees and his arms raise up, light as helium without the weight of his daughter to hold them, and it's like he's genuflecting. But no, Nova knows it's worthless, this gesture. She knows there's nothing out there past the clouds he's tilted his face up to. How the fuck can there be? How the fuck can there be a god to drop to your knees in front of in a world—in a moment—that lets you dump your little girl over the side of some dumb fucking carnival ride? But he's down there, low. Low like Nova's insides. A heaviness in her gut, a force greater than gravity keeps her pressed in on her side of the cage, pressed in tight between the bony shoulders of Michael, the broad ones of Sky, pressed against the back of their seat, against vinyl against metal. And the ride keeps turning, and maybe it's that centrifugal stuff, you know, like water in a swinging bucket, because Nova can't budge, she's held in solid and sure (and high, so very, very high) in the cage, in the air, in this tight, tight moment. Did it really happen? And for just a split of second, Nova thinks—no hopes, almost prays (but of course she won't) that it didn't really happen. It smells so good up here, after all. Like corndogs and cotton candy and freshly mowed lawns. Smells too good for anything bad. Smells safe, see? And they're high, after all, she and Michael and Sky; and they're kids. You know. Kids who are prone to imagining things. Only there's the wife, the mother, up in an instant and gaping, eyes and mouth wide, wide circles, lips moving. But no sound, no sound. And Nova can't help but marvel at how deeply silent the world is, all empty, safe-smelling air and sudden stillness. And the sky past the useless bars is so blue it hurts to look at it in the silence. But it's just that one silent instant before they hear it as the baby bounces off of the other cages, off of the solid, unforgiving spokes of the stupid ride—a big old Ferris wheel type thing, too big for the small town, for the little carnival, for the dinky midway and especially too, too big for that tiny, tiny girl who makes (not with her mouth but with her body) the same exact sound after sound all the way down. A sound too horrific to be replicated, but a sound that splat and smacked its way into the souls of them all left behind on the still-moving ride, a sound that played itself over and over in the dreams of Nova that night and, she would swear to it, each and every night forever after.

And then the screams come. From below at first, from those riders under them getting it finally, seeing that hurtling thing for what it is, not the doll that some of them must have thought, but a little girl at first, reaching and grabbing at the air and catching nothing except maybe some eyes here and there, some bright panicked eyes locked with hers. And then, merci-fully, the little girl becomes just a body, dead and all, long (long, long seconds) before she hits the ground.

When Nova opens her own eyes—she hadn't known she'd closed them—she stares at her hands in her lap, the good one with all five nails polished deep purple and pointy, and the other one. And then she sees the mom drop to her knees beside the dad (arms still raised) and then onto her belly so she can stretch her hands out through the bottom of the bars, reach for what she can no longer have, and Nova feels her own hands clutch, feels her one strong fist and feels the other one, stunted from birth, its tiny pink thumb all by itself tightening and holding on. And when the mom knows what's true, knows that's the end of it, she writhes on the floor and howls and the dad does, too, and they're both down there, together, all they have left, and they braid into one another, one long rope of two bodies and a single, twining, rattling wail rising from them.

"Holy fuck." It's Sky who talks first. They are all squeezed in so tight together there, the three of them (brother, sister, friend) that Nova feels the words rumbling up from his body, feels the hollow breath of them on her shoulder. And she nods. And then the ride stops, a sudden, screeching jolt of movement halted. They rock forward and back in their seat and it's Michael, the friend, who finally acts. He's down there, too, on the floor between the seats at Nova's, at Sky's feet, all coos and rubbing and holding, and it's like he's left them, Nova and Sky, deserted them for these strangers. Like he has become one of the shattered family. And when he pulls these parents to him he's much more than a kid, more than fourteen; he's like some grownup now or something, some large being, bigger than Nova has ever seen him, and the three of *them* rock there together, holding and crying and shushing and patting, and the mother reaches for the dad and Michael is there in the middle and he kisses them, one then the other, on their heads, on their arms. And they cling to him.

"Damn, Mike, what the fuck?" Sky says, and Nova wants to slug him. Not like she usually does, not like the way all sisters want to slug their brothers, but she wants to hit him in such a way as to really hurt him. She wants to make him ache throughout. She wants him to feel some pain, some deep, numbing pain. Like the one she feels filling her chest, pushing at her throat. But Sky's snickering now, and nudging her in the ribs with an elbow, whispering, "Copping a little feel there, you ask me." And it's too much for Nova. All way, way, way too much. So she slides as far from him as she can across the scarred vinyl of the bench (impossibly wide now with just Nova, small Nova, little for her thirteen years and big, thick, golden-haired Sky on it) and she turns and presses her forehead against the ice-cold bars and something lifts from the murkiness of her gut, from that low, heavy feeling that keeps her down, keeps her seated. Something rises up and through her and she gives into its rise, and she opens her mouth and lets it come. And first it's a sound, something deep and unrecognizable. Wild. And then it's something else. Something thicker. And she works to throw it up, this thickness. But even as she pukes and pukes and pukes, she can't get rid of it. And she knows that. Even as she continues to try to free herself, moaning and crying and purging, Nova knows that this is something that will always, always be there inside of her. Something raw and hot and over-whelming. Something like faith.

The story was built at the kitchen table. Nova tried to listen as Sky recreated the scene for their mother, but it was as though she were underwater. His words, muffled by a rush in her ears, sounded round somehow, and empty as bubbles.

"They were going crazy, the mom and dad," he said. And he took a large bite of his tuna sandwich. How could he eat? Nova wondered. How could anyone, anywhere, ever keep anything down again?

Their mother tsked, wrung her hands.

Sky talked through his mouthful. "I couldn't just watch it, you know. I had to do something."

Nova's head swam. She crossed her hands, the good over the bad, on the table, and rested a cheek on her knuckles. The tablecloth smelled of cooking smoke and mayonnaise. Her stomach roiled. Her mouth filled with saliva, the sting of bile. She wished she were still high.

"So what did you do?" Their mother asked. Like it was the first time she heard the story. Sky was making his way through it for what, the third?, fourth? time, the encores encouraged by their mom. She lived for this stuff, this crisis and courage, death and transcendence. She nodded her son on. And Nova couldn't help but notice, and not for the first time, how much mother and son resembled one another. And Nova, small and bleached near to invisible in the light of the big, golden-haired couple, looked like the outsider. Their mother fingered a small metal cross in the hollow above her heart.

The story had become Sky's own. He took the part of Michael, his friend, made himself a hero. He sat up tall in his seat, put his sandwich on the paper plate in front of him, wiped at his mouth with the back of his hand. "Well," he said. He cleared his throat, gave a quick glance in Nova's direction. Her hair fell in platinum sheets before her face, made a curtain between herself and her family. She knew he couldn't see her eyes. "I didn't want to tell you this at first, Mom. Just in case you might get mad."

The older woman leaned forward in her seat, her hands flat on the table, nailbitten fingertips reaching toward her son.

"Go on," she said.

"The mom was hysterical—as you can imagine. Crying. Screaming. So I—" Sky paused, Nova tried hard to hear through the rush in her ears. "I slapped her, Mom."

Their mother fell back in her seat like she was pushed, like those people on the televangelist shows do when the preacher releases his grip on their foreheads. Nova stood up.

"Enough," she said—or thought she did, she couldn't be sure the word actually came out of the wetness that was her mouth. Sky went on talking.

"And then the ambulance came," he said. "And of course I rode with them." Sky's story faltered here since it was Michael who had actually gone off in the ambulance. It was Michael who had helped the weeping parents off the floor and back onto their seat on the other side of the wide-barred cage, Michael who held them in place as the ride made its full circle and they were finally allowed to stand on pavement. Michael who clutched their hands and patted their backs as they fell to their knees next to the broken little body while Nova and Sky lost themselves in the crowd so when the cops got there they wouldn't be pointed out and wouldn't have to explain what happened or how it happened (like anyone could explain that) and why their eyes were red and their hair reeking. And they wouldn't be asked to empty their pockets: "Just a formality." And since they weren't around when the ambulance came and Michael left them, that was all of the story Sky knew for sure. He'd need some time to figure out his own ending, a better one than he'd come up with so far.

"It was just so horrible after that. And sad," he looked at his mother again, and then at Nova, like he'd just noticed her standing there. He shook his head, and made a slight wink in her direction. Nova flinched. "I just can't talk about it," Sky said.

"Enough," Nova said for real this time. Mother and brother turned up to her, and Nova swooned, her whole body a wave. She gripped the edge of the table and looked down into the wide, blue-eyed, upturned faces of her family. "Enough," she said again when she felt herself steady, and she turned from the pair and left the house. The screen door banged against its jamb and Nova stepped under the porch light and into a sea of tiny flying things, and then she was running into the dark and away from her home, from the lies, from her brother calling "Wait! Wait!" trapped by his own story in his own kitchen in the audience of his (and her) own mother.

The blacktopped road back to town was spongy from the heat, even though an hour had passed since the sun set. Nova breathed in the summer night. She wanted the waterlogged feeling in her head to go away, she wanted to think of something other than what happened, other than Sky making the story even more horrible (could it possibly be?) to impress their mother. The thing was, though, Nova's mother believed this stuff. She believed most anything that had to do with heroes and faith, with saviors and those in need of salvation. But Nova couldn't stomach this kind of blind devotion, the unwillingness to question, the absolute submission. At least not anymore. Not since she'd been duped that one time, long ago, into letting God enter her life.

Sky and his dad (her dad) were newly back in town then.

Up until that time, Nova had come to believe she didn't have a father. Her mother was cryptic and prayerful in her answer to Nova's questions ("the Lord works in mysterious ways,") so Nova couldn't help but imagine an immaculate conception of sorts. When, at ten years old, Nova found out that she actually did have a dad, a real, flesh and blood one, and she had a twelve-year-old brother, too, it was like remembering the words to a song whose tune had been playing over and over in her head so long she barely even noticed it anymore. The two of them, father and son, had come full of apologies and ripe with stories, and at the heart of each of those was the word of God. Nova supposed that's why her mother let them in, probably why she'd said yes when her father proposed. ("Finally," she whispered to Nova when they stood at the back of the tiny church on the day of the wedding.)

Sky could talk the word of God better than anyone; back then, he even believed it himself. He had the gift, their father said, a direct connection to the absolute truth. Pretty soon Sky started having Bible study meetings in their living room, the place filled with kids from the elementary and middle schools, a few from the high school. Nova sat at the feet of her new big brother and listened to him tell stories of the places he'd been all over the Midwest. From Clinton to Mount Vernon, Milwaukee to Normal. He told of sick children on the road to recovery, of families pulled apart and brought back together. Here he'd always look down into Nova's eyes, and smile a smile that made her face burn.

"All you need to do is ask," Sky would say. "Ask God into your life. Ask him to protect you, to save you. He'll come, you'll see. The Father always comes when the children need him. When they are ready to receive him. Let your Father know that you are ready." And of course, Nova couldn't help but think of the return of her own father, there suddenly in her life just when she needed him, there to protect her from the unrelenting boredom of the small town, the dumb, undirected faith of her mother. Like some sort of hero he'd swept in and carried her off in his dusty pickup, just the three of them, Nova, Sky, Father, and they'd driven the gravel roads of New Hope to the lake where he held her hands, both of them, and walked her out into the water and dunked her head and pronounced her newly born—now of the Father. And before then, Nova might have believed in God, but it was similar to riding a bicycle, her belief: something everyone did without thinking about it. Simple and unremarkable. But this child and Father reunion thing, Nova knew was something else. Something better. Like riding a bike without using your hands. Or feet, maybe. Like riding on air.

So she tried it. That night after the lake she laid still and silent in her twin bed, squeezed her eyes closed so tightly her forehead hurt. In her mind, and in her heart, too, she prayed. Not the usual stuff: *Now I lay me down to sleep*; *The Lord is my shepherd*; *Bless us, O Lord...* This time Nova spoke, she was pretty sure, directly to God. "Save me," she said. "I'm ready. I'm finally ready." She stretched herself long and taut and steadied herself as if preparing for a blow. She listened to her breath in the dark, she squinted into the darkness so hard it began to swirl. And then he came. She felt it. A bright whooshing sensation ran over her and through her, a wash of something cold and hot at the very same time. A feeling like panic and excitement, like joy and terror. She shuddered under the sweep of it. She nearly screamed. But she kept quiet and held tight to her sheets and rode it out under the blanket for the seconds (minutes?) it lasted. And when it passed, Nova's whole body tingled. And then she was asleep.

Later that night, something woke her. A noise, perhaps. The quiet bleat of a car horn, a door closing. And in that moment of blurred awareness, Nova felt a fat lump in her throat, a hollow pain in her chest. She thought it must be God still, working her over, having his way. But in the morning she was fevered and sore throughout, stricken with the flu. And at the breakfast table her mother was crying and Sky wouldn't look up from his cornflakes and Nova knew that the father was gone.

Headlights came around the bend in the road ahead of her. Nova stuck tight to the shoulder, as close to the weeds as she could get without stepping into the opening of the ditch. A white sedan slowed as it passed, a four-door family car, and Nova nodded when the old guy lifted a small finger in a wave and drove on. She wondered if maybe she were dreaming. It felt like it. Not the whole day, she knew what happened on The Gondolier was real, she could still hear that body-against-machine sound in her ears. But maybe this was a dream. This walking in the dark like she walked through water. It felt like it does in dreams, legs and arms moving in slow, slow motion. She lifted her hands up in front of her face and studied them in the light of the full moon. She wasn't dreaming. In her dreams she always had two perfectly formed hands.

She passed the occasional farm or trailer set back from the road. Some shone in the bright spot of an outdoor security light. Others, dark on the outside, had wide-open windows that flashed with the pulse of nighttime TV. Evidence of life. The night sounded around Nova, crickets and frogs in the ditch mixed it up with the far away plastic noise of laugh tracks and sirens.

The smell of skunk filled the air, and Nova breathed deeply. She loved the smell of skunk. Ahead in the road there was a dark lump with its unmistakable stripe glowing white in the moonlight. Nova looked both ways down the long, flat plane of road before she stepped onto the pavement and up to the body. Right over the thing like this, the smell was almost unpleasant. Too much of a good thing. But as she breathed the sharp odor, Nova felt the rushing behind her eyes ease, felt her limbs pull out from the weight of whatever it was that had held her. She knelt on the road next to the body and pressed her tiny hand against a spot on its tail where there was more fur than open flesh and blood. After a minute, she lifted her hand to her face. There it was, the thick, sharp, wonderful smell on her small, pink palm, on her perfect, miniature thumb. Satisfied and clear-headed, Nova stood up and continued her walk into town.

"Mmm, skunk." The words came from the rear of the HiLo Foods parking lot, and even before she saw him there in their usual spot, Nova knew it was Michael, the only other person she'd ever known to like the smell. She made her way to him and held out her hand so he could get a whiff. "Mm-mm," he said and breathed deeply.

Above them, the neon HiLo sign made its quiet hum; its light bathed the lot in a watery blue. Nova sat down on the blacktop where Michael crouched low and tight against the wall. He didn't look good. His eyes were red and shiny, his face blotchy and streaked with grime. He sniffled, wiped his nose with the cuff of his flannel shirt. He was shaking.

"Cold, man, don't you think?" Nova nodded even though it was at least eighty out still, and her neck and back were slick with sweat.

"How are you?" She asked. It wasn't what she meant to say, but it was all she could come up with.

Michael nodded. He lifted a bottle in a brown paper sack from between his knees, swallowed hard, then shook it in her direction. "Some?"

Nova took the bottle and swigged. She had to fight down the wet burn of the booze, had to give her throat and stomach and head time to get used to it, to recognize this feeling as something different, something better than the boiling that had filled her before. With the second swallow, she felt a knot in the back of her neck loosen.

"Where's Sky?" Michael asked. He wouldn't look at Nova, instead he stared at a dark spot of something on the back of his hand. Blood, maybe.

"Not sure. Home? Probably not, though. My mom must've let him loose by now."

"He in trouble?"

"You kidding? Sky? The golden boy?" Nova slugged on the bottle again. She passed it back to Michael who, instead of drinking, held the bottle, his fingers working its neck, wringing it. "Nah, Sky's not in trouble. He's never in trouble. You know how he is. Too slick for getting into trouble." She laughed a little. "Nah, Mom's just all over him cause of what happened." Nova paused, she wondered if she should tell Michael that Sky had taken his story away. He was always doing things like that, taking things from Michael—his silver lighter, his ten-speed, his leather jacket. Nova thought maybe that's why Sky let Michael, a skinny, loner of a kid a year behind him in school, hang around. She leaned back against the bricks of the grocery store. Inside they had started the baking for the next day. The warm, full smell of fresh bread came out of the exhaust vent above their heads. "Skunk and bread," Nova said and inhaled with her whole body. "This must be heaven."

"Or hell," Michael said. He drank from the bottle again, swiped his nose, rubbed his palms over his eyes. "Fuck it, man." He looked her dead on, blue eyes gleaming. "Got any weed?"

"Matter of fact," Nova reached into the breast pocket of her T-shirt, pulled out a skinny little joint, the one she'd been saving for when they got off the carnival wheel that afternoon. The one she'd hoped would help her get her land legs back.

Michael struck a match against the wall, and they huddled around the glow of it. Nova sucked deeply and watched how Michael's eyes flecked gold with the match light. She held the smoke in, her chest full, her shoulders lifted, and passed the joint.

"Thanks," he said, and leaned his head back. He smoked towards the moon.

It went like that for a while. Drag and pass, drag and pass. Joint, bottle, joint, bottle. Nova waited. Something should be happening soon. She should feel fucked up. Michael should say something. Something, something, something. A car moved quietly down the street in front of the store. A dog barked a block away, another one answered. Nova stayed painfully sober.

"Want this?" Michael held the stub of roach out towards Nova. She shook her head so he popped it into his mouth and swallowed. "Lemme smell that hand," he said. His breath felt hot and damp on her shrunken palm. When he'd got enough of the skunk, Michael held her hand in his lap. For as far back as Nova could remember, no one else had ever held her bad hand like that. Like it was just a hand. Like it was meant to be held. She thought then, and wasn't entirely surprised by the thought, that maybe she loved Michael.

"Hey," she said.

"Hmm?" He stroked his thumb up and down her tiny one. His face looked white and blue in the moonlight and neon. Luminescent, she thought. He blinked heavily.

"You're fucked up."

"Thank God."

Nova let that pass.

A couple strolled along the sidewalk at the front of the grocery store's parking lot. They each had a hand pushed into the back pocket of the other's jeans.

"Pretty late for a walk," Nova said. It was probably not yet midnight, but in the small town nothing was open past ten-thirty.

"Gawkers," Michael said. "Rubber necks."

"What?"

"You know, like when you slow down on the road 'cause there's a cop there with his lights on. Like how we watch that war stuff on the news. Want to see the villains, the dead. In this case, the scene of the crime."

"What're you talking about?"

"Been going on all night. People going down to the midway on Main. Checking out where the kid fell. The big wheel. Putting their hands on the yellow police tape."

"There's police tape?"

"Yup."

Nova let the TV-ness of the whole thing sink in. Yellow tape, gawkers—she looked at the dark spot on Michael's hand—blood.

"How'd you know what to do, Michael?" Nova asked.

"Whaddaya mean?"

"You know, up there." She lifted her chin as though she were pointing to the top of the wheel. "How'd you know how to do the right thing?"

"I didn't."

"I was there, Michael, remember? Yes, you did. You knew exactly what to do."

"Don't make me out a hero here, Nova." He looked at her, pushed a fine strand of her hair behind one of her ears. "I mean it." His lips drew into a tight line.

"Sky's the hero at home," she said. "He's telling my mom he did all those things you did. It's his story now."

"Good. Let him have it."

"But you should be proud, Michael—"

"Look!" Michael said and let go of Nova's hand. He pushed himself up from the ground, kicked the empty bottle across the lot. It shattered against a parking curb. "I didn't do anything, see? I didn't do anything!" He turned away from Nova, and she saw his shoulders shake. She waited a second before she stood up next to him and put her good hand on the small of his back. She could feel the knobs of his spine. "Don't you get it?" He said, his voice wobbly and wet. "That's why I had to do what I did when I did. I didn't do anything earlier." Michael swabbed at his face with the back of his hand then hugged himself with both arms crossed over his chest. "I saw it coming, don't you see? I saw it coming." He cried hard now, his whole body pummeled by the sobs. "I should have said something. I mean, what was I thinking? It made me sick to my stomach to watch it, the guy letting his little girl fly around the place like that. It was just waiting to happen. I should have said something. But I didn't. I was afraid, I guess. Tried to mind my own fucking business. Shit, I don't know. Maybe I was too embarrassed to say anything. I mean, who was I to tell a grownup what to do? Just a kid. A fucked up fucking kid. So I just turned my head. I ignored it."

Nova didn't want to hear this. She'd watched the guy, too, swinging his little girl and all. Only to her, it looked nice how the baby laid there stretched out in the cradle of his arms. Innocent. Something she wanted to watch, to be part of. How could Michael see the same, exact thing and see something so entirely different?

"Damnit, how could I ignore it? I mean, I'm sure the guy must've thought he had a good grip there, but let's face it, if a kid wants to get loose from its father, how hard is that? I must have done it a million times when I was little. You must have done it." The more Michael talked, the more Nova wanted to stop him, to yell at him to shut up, to close his Goddamn mouth.

"Son of a bitch! Stupid, worthless, mother fucker!" He was yelling now, and he punched the wall once, twice. Then, almost too quiet to hear, "Damnit, why didn't I say something? I should have said something." He rested his forehead against the building and bent at the knees and slid down to the ground again. His head scraped and bumped over the bricks. He looked up at Nova. There was blood in his bangs, purple in the blue light, but he didn't seem to notice. "So I had to do what I did, because I didn't do what I should. Now do you get it? I'm no fucking hero, Nova. Sky wants to be one, fine. Me, I'm just trying to survive it."

Why did he have to tell her this? Couldn't he see he was spoiling everything? Why couldn't he just be a hero and be happy? Why couldn't he let her be happy? Why did he have to ruin it all?

"You need to go back there," she heard herself say.

"What? No fucking way."

"No really," and it was like things were spinning out of her mouth, advice and shit that she'd heard somewhere, on television or something, or maybe one of Sky's meetings. "Like when those people all got killed in that plane crash, remember?" She didn't have any particular plane crash in mind, there was a new one every year or so, but Michael nodded at her like he knew just what she was talking about. "Or that restaurant where all those people got killed when the roof fell in. Or those guys in the war." He nodded again. "Remember how all those people— the survivors—went back to those places where those terrible things happened? And when they went back, then—" and here she reached both hands out to him to help him stand—"and only then, did those people really get past it." A load of crap, she knew. But something made her want to take Michael back to where the thing had happened. She wanted him to see the place again. She wanted him to feel it all again. She wanted him to pay for what he'd done to her by telling her his story.

At the foot of the ramp to The Gondolier, the couple they'd seen on the street hugged one another. The woman had her face buried in the shirtfront of the man; he stared over her head and into the center of the big wheel. On the ground all around the ride were small placements of flowers and stuffed animals. A three-foot cross made from tinfoil and cardboard leaned against the ticket booth. "$1.00" a sign above the booth's window read. And another one misspelled in marker: "Plese Hold Onto You're Valubles." The flowers had begun to bake in the hot night air, and the place was ripe with the rotting smell of garbage. Street lamps along Main Street threw uneven pools of light on the dark carnival attractions. Nova stopped Michael in the shadows of the ring toss tent.

"Wait," she said. "When they go." She could feel Michael shaking next to her, his teeth chattered. "You'll be fine," she said, and when she heard a certain edge in her voice, she reached out for his hand, made herself raise his scraped knuckles to her lips. "You'll be fine," she said again softly against his fingers.

It seemed as though the couple had no intention of ever leaving their spot. Nova watched them pressed together, the gigantic, unmoving wheel behind them, and pushed against the flooded feeling that rose again inside her. "Why don't they go?" She whispered sharply and looked at Michael. His face streamed with tears, his chest heaved under his flannel shirt. Nova could hear the quiet hiccup of his sobs. Something softened in her, and she was just about to say that maybe they'd had enough for one day when the couple moved on and was replaced by a dark figure. A slow, stumbling man walked with an unsteady purpose to the spot that was wound round and round with the yellow police tape. A spot Nova just then recognized as where the body—or most of it at least, wouldn't it have split apart on impact?—must have landed. The man went down on all fours and crawled beneath the plastic barriers. He rested a cheek on the ground and didn't move. It was like he was listening to the workings of the world.

"Fucking drunk," Nova said. "What nerve." She started out from under the shadows, but Michael held fast to her hand.

"No," he said.

She shook him off and headed for the man.

"Hey! Asshole!" Nova yelled.

The man looked up, and as she got closer, Nova began to make out his face, began to sense a familiarity.

"You," the man said, but it was like he was in a daze, the word came out soft as a prayer. He looked not at Nova, but over her shoulder, beyond her.

"Holy shit," she said when she put the man, the place, and the dead girl together. She spun around and found Michael trotting towards her. "It's the guy," she said. "It's the father."

"Yes," Michael said and tried to grab Nova's arm. "Let's give him some privacy."

She shrugged out from Michael's reach and looked back at the man. "No," she said. And then again, "No."

And then, without premeditation, Nova felt herself launch into a full-out charge. Michael moved behind her, but she was way ahead of him. She broke through the police tape and felt herself land on the man, felt him fall back with the weight of her, felt his skin under her fists as she pounded on his face, on his neck. And again, it was as if she were dreaming, only this was like that dream she had where she would be beating someone, her mother maybe, or Sky, or someone else, and no matter how hard she hit, she couldn't make them feel it. The man's face came into focus beneath her hands. His eyes flashed with surprise, but behind that was something else. Something muddy and impenetrable.

Hands circled her ankles, and Nova knew that Michael had caught up. She tried to kick him away, but he held fast. The funny thing was, the man lay still while she hit him for what felt like forever to Nova. When Michael had a good enough grip to pull her down the length of the man's body, it was as though he slowly came to. He blinked and blinked, and with a jerky momentum, the man tried to catch Nova's fists. He latched onto the bad hand, the smelly one, and when he held it in front of his face, Nova saw all that she hated to see. First his lips pulled back and he bared his teeth against the odor of the skunk, and then she saw him flinch when he recognized that he held only part of a hand. And, worst of all, his eyes widened with that look that Nova long ago (about the time of her father's departure) decided was pity. He opened up his mouth as though he were going to say something, and in that moment Nova planned to break his fucking teeth in if he dared to tell her he was sorry.

"Goddamnit, Nova!" Michael had her by the waist now and swung her up and over his shoulder. She hated being such a little girl. "Leave the guy alone."

Nova slugged at Michael's back, flailed her legs as hard as she could against his chest.

"Put me down, you dickhead! Put me the fuck down!" She was screaming now, the words scraped her throat, rattled her chest. Michael bobbled under her. "Shh, shh," he was saying, a loud spray of sound. "Let me go!" She could see from where she hung over Michael's back the man stand up and brush himself off, she saw him move in their direction. Her head rushed with heat and blood and her body seethed.

"Stay away from me!" She yelled at the father. "I'll kill you, you mother fucker!" It was a wonder Michael could hang onto her. "I'll kill you, you mother fucker! I'll kill you! Mother fucker! Fucker! Mother fucker!"

And then she felt Michael fold beneath her and felt herself pushed from him. When she scrambled to her knees, Nova recognized Sky's broad shoulders and golden curls. She saw the pulling back of his arm, the release and swing repeated again and again. Michael's face rolled side to side, more bloodied with each punch from Sky. Nova crawled toward them. Michael looked at Nova through swollen eyes, his lips moved, his mouth opened. "Gaaahhh," he said. Crimson muck spilled over his teeth. "Gaahhh." It was like he was speaking right to her; Nova strained to hear. "Gaahh…" or maybe it was "God." Or maybe: "Good."

"He hurt you?" Sky asked. His voice was calm. He kept his eyes on Michael's face. A white smudge of mayonnaise marked his cheek and Nova felt a stinging desire to wipe it away, to hold her brother's head in her hands. Her protector, her hero, the only one she had. But Nova couldn't make herself move and Sky continued to beat his friend, his hands, raw and blood-covered, traveling from the head to the chest and back up to the face. He had Michael's arms pinned under his knees even though Michael wasn't struggling. "You okay, Novie?" Sky asked in that calm voice. Nova nodded. It was like Michael was letting this happen to himself, like he wasn't even trying to stop it. And Sky kept at it with a controlled rhythm: beat, beat, beat. Nova believed her brother was doing this for her; she had to. This had nothing to do with Michael, what he'd done, what Sky had not. This, Nova told herself, was about Sky and Nova. Of course it was.

Michael's head lolled back and forth, each blow the sound of meat slammed against meat. He spit blood and something else, broken tooth maybe, then coughed and gurgled. Nova wasn't able to look away from her brother's heroics, even as she heard the man come up behind them.

"Holy Mother of God," the man said. "That's enough now, don't you think? You should stop now." Even still, the man stayed back, watched the beating alongside Nova. "Stop it now, son. You're killing him, son."

"Yes," Nova said and looked away from the hero and up at the man. She saw under his eye a small patch the size of the nail on her miniature thumb. She smiled up at the father. "Yes," she said again, her chest thick and aching with pride. "He is."

Just Like That

Officially it was senior prom, but Arnie said it was more like a regular party when you think about it, but a going away party with a bunch of kids we didn't like that much all dressed up and crying and hugging—and why would he want any part of that? Not like any of us were going all that far away; mostly we were just heading down the road to Highland Community College for a couple of years, and okay, some were going into the army, and maybe to Vietnam, who knew for certain. But still.

Arnie was the only one who was really going far—a full scholarship to something-I-T out East, a place that was tailor-made for a guy like him. You know, brilliant. Not that nerdy kind of brilliant, physics and algorithms—although he was great at that too—but a different kind of genius. The kind that could sort through all the crap and find the threads, the connections, the way everything could—if you looked at it just right and put it in some kind of order—make sense somehow.

Still, it was prom night, the only one either one of us would ever get a chance to go to, and I did sort of want to go. Don't ask me why. Maybe because it was a rite of passage, you know, something to mark a specific time in our lives. Or it could have been because I was one of those kids who was going away. I guess I'm sort of smart as well, because I got a scholarship, too, only across the river to a state university. No big deal, but my first time anywhere at all really, besides here. Here, New Hope, which is a small town you probably never even heard of before. Or maybe you did, after that night, the night of the prom. Still, even if you've heard of it, it's the kind of place that's not too hard to forget. Which, when I think about it, was another reason I thought it might be fun to go to prom. A way of remembering.

So I talked Arnie into it, like I can talk him into a lot of things. Like skitching. You know, when you grab the back of a car, the bumper, and it's icy out, and you hold on and the car pulls away, slow at first, but if it's your friends driving and they know you're doing it, they'll go pretty fast pretty quick, and next thing you know they're pulling doughnuts in the parking lot of Jack's new Super HiLo, and you're swirling on the ice, holding on for dear life and feeling your heart right up there near your ears. It's great. Really. But Arnie, brilliant as he is, could see all the things that could go wrong with a situation like this—which is exactly why it's so fun—and it took some convincing for him to try it. He did though, maybe because I said he didn't have to, I'd go off with Derek Jerabek and do it, and Derek and Arnie had this feud so old and deep that I don't know if they knew what was behind it anymore. Anyway, the next night Arnie's right there with me at Jack's Super, waiting his turn to grab a bumper, and he's wearing his Converses, the best kind of skitching shoe, all slick and thin in the sole. And when it's his turn, Arnie won't let go, he's riding that bumper like a cowboy on a bull, hanging on and hollering. And it's Derek behind the wheel and he's pulling one-eighties and three-sixties and figure eights. But Arnie holds on. And finally Derek has to stop so someone else can have a turn to get on board, and Arnie's face is frozen in this loopy grin, and I have to help him peel his hands off the bumper, one finger at a time, and his sneakers have worn clear through in places, and he's hyped, I mean, hyped like I've never seen him before and he wants to go again, right away, but his fingers aren't straightening up and his fingertips are blue, so I talk him into coming home with me for a little while to warm up, which he does but only when I promise we'll go right back out. We get to my house and I'm sort of worried, his hands are so cold and not just his shoes but his socks have holes, too, and I blow on his hands and rub his feet, and he's talking that talk guys do when they're excited, you know: "That was so fucking cool! Did you see that? Did you see me on Derek like that? Shit!" And I want him to shut up because, like I say, I'm worried, he's so cold, so when he tries to pull away from me I decide to switch gears and get his attention, and so I pull his hand toward me and slide it up under my sweater and onto my warm belly—and it's so cold, his hand, but I hold it there and try not to let my teeth chatter. And Arnie shuts up, just like that, silent as a block of ice, and looks at me, and I put his other hand under my sweater too, and then slide it under my belt, down where it's really warm, and we lay back on my bed and I get him under the covers and we're both shivering but we just stare at one another a while until his hands get warm and his breath goes heavy.

It's not like this is the first time we did anything like that. I mean, we grew up right next door to one another, so we used to play *You show me yours, I'll show you mine* when we were kids. And when we got to junior high, we were best friends, and one time I had this crush on this guy Sky Spalding. He was in our grade, but a little older than the rest of us, a new kid who got held back because they were moving all the time, and they moved again a couple years after all this I'm going to tell you happened. I still remember how he had these great greeny-blue eyes. And once he asked me to sit back in the stacks with him in the library and he was back there with Derek, and we were all just sitting there and talking when all of a sudden this guy Sky says he knows that I like him and would it be okay if we Frenched. Well, I could feel my stomach knot up, I was so excited, my first time French kissing anyone, and here it was, Sky with the green-blue eyes. So I nodded, feeling a bit shy, too, maybe because Derek was there. And so Sky leans over and puts his lips against mine and sticks his tongue out and it feels sort of stiff and tastes like—I'll never forget this—salami, and he just holds it there and wiggles his head around, and I've got my eyes closed and am waiting for it to feel like something special, and I hear Derek over there snort or something, and I open my eyes, and even though Sky is kissing me, he's giving Derek this sidelong glance. And then Sky pulls his head back and wipes his hand over his mouth, and he says, "You're good," and even though I don't know how this could possibly be, I mean I just opened my mouth and let his tongue in, I'm feeling a bit proud about that. And then he puts his hand on my neck and just like that slides it right down the front of my blouse and inside my bra and squeezes my tit in his hand, once, twice, and Derek is there still, wide-eyed and open mouthed, and I feel sick in my stomach for so many reasons I can't even begin to sort them out. I want to pull Sky's hand right back out of there, but that seems like the wrong thing to do for some reason, like after I already was there for the kiss and all, could I really back off now? And Sky's hand is rough and sort of sweaty, and pretty soon he pulls it out himself and I'm just sitting there not knowing exactly what to do or say, but smiling a little like it's all okay, no big deal, but I feel my face is burning, and my scalp is starting to prickle. And when Sky and Derek swap a glance at one another, lift their eyebrows, I excuse myself, say I have to go somewhere or something, and I walk away as casually as I can, and I can feel their Goddamned eyes on the back of my jeans, and I go to the girls room and lean over the sink and look at my face which I suspect has changed, but it's the same, really, only I think a little sad looking. And later, at home while I'm baby-sitting the twins and Arnie comes over I want to tell him about it, because I feel like I should tell someone, I'm sort of excited even though I'm still feeling a little something else I haven't yet figured out. But Arnie already knows, that's the way it is in a town like this, nothing is a secret for very long, especially when it comes to boys, and he looks sort of mad standing there in the door, and so I tell him my side—he already knew about the crush on Sky—and here's the funny thing. When I tell him, I start to cry, who knows why that is, but I do a little, and Arnie's holding me like he has once or twice before, like when my folks got divorced, like when my dad died, and then I'm really crying. So Arnie asks what can he do, and I think about that, and I figure out that I want him to kiss me, to touch my boob, because I know that with him it will be different, nice, caring—friendly, I guess—and so he does, only he's a little nervous at first, his hand is shaking, but he's warm and his tongue is wet and soft and his hand is smooth and we stay there like that for a long while, the two of us on my couch, the twins napping in the next room, and he just leaves his hand on my breast like that, and when his tongue slips in and out of my mouth, I taste it with my own tongue and it's sweet, milky, and we both get a little fogged up, and I'm not crying anymore, but more like floating. And after a few minutes of this, he stops, pulls away, and looks at me. His glasses are steamed. He says, "Better?" and his voice is rough. And I nod and rearrange my top, my bra. And Arnie says, "Good," and he gets up and goes to the kitchen and gets us a Pepsi which we pass back and forth, not saying anything else.

And every once in a while since then, we would come together like this, fiddle around a little. It wasn't about sex, I don't think, even though our teachers and folks kept reminding us how our hormones were going crazy and we'd have to be careful. I guess we loved one another, when you think about it, but in a friendly way, in a way that has to do with knowing each other better than we knew anybody else on the planet. So it wasn't about lust, but it wasn't exactly about love, either. It was more about something else. Like what I was saying about Arnie's brilliance, about connections and making sense of the big picture. That's it, I think.

So of course it made sense that we should go to prom together. And we were in my back yard taking turns behind the lawn-mower and talking about the dance. Well, I was talking about it, trying to make my point to Arnie, who just nodded and looked away over the back fence and squeezed my dog King's chewed-up rubber ball in his hand. And the twins, Jimmy and Jerry, who were seven, were ahead of us supposedly picking up twigs and toys and sticks and things, but mostly just picking up King's dog doo with plastic bags on their hands like mittens, and they'd pretend to throw it at each other before dropping it into the bag they carried.

"Tell me again why you think we should go," Arnie said, and the mower roared between us, and the twins screamed and laughed and ran in circles, and the cicadas made that electric noise they make when it gets hot. It was just May, but eighty out, and it sounded like summer already.

"Come on, Arnie," I said and pounded on the mower's handle. "What's the big deal? It's just a few hours out of your life, and besides, it might be fun."

Arnie snorted in that superior way of his that he reserved for teachers who had a hard time keeping up with his answers to their questions. I watched the muscle in his forearm tense and release as he squeezed the ball, watched the little blue vein over his wrist pop up.

"Okay, think of it this way," I said as we turned back toward the house, making another line in the grass, "it's a favor to me.

You might not feel like this, but I think that if I don't go, I'll regret it somehow. Maybe not right away, but you know, years from now, when I'm old, and I'm thinking back over things."

Arnie hated it when I talked like this, about growing old, which I do a lot for some reason. He called himself a "fatalist," like it was something he should be proud of like his having a high IQ was. He always thought an end—some end, who knows?—was near. I thought we'd both grow remarkably old, break records like those people who ate yogurt in Siberia. Maybe live forever.

"If it sucks," I said, and Arnie said, "Which it will," and I went on like I hadn't heard, "we can change the night and leave. If we don't go, we can't change things. We just won't have gone. Period." And I was pleased with myself, because I knew Arnie got what I meant, and it was almost one of those brilliant things he might say.

We were closing in on the last few swipes across the lawn, and the twins had tossed aside their bag and were rolling around with King now, whose tongue was hanging out and dripping in the heat. Mom and Mrs. Lawlor, Arnie's mom, were on the patio drinking sun tea and listening to the radio. They both were frowning, and Mrs. Lawlor shook her head. When I got closer, I could hear enough of what was being said to know it had to do with the war. Arnie was still near the back fence, staring out across the field. I saw him nod his head a little, like he was talking to himself like he sometimes does, and then I saw him hurl King's ball as hard as he could towards—well, it was all flat, vacant field back there. Under the right conditions, that ball could roll for miles.

So we went to prom. And I thought Arnie's mom might burst when we left, the way she looked so proud and was snapping all these pictures and talking about how she couldn't wait until Arnie's dad came home later that week (he traveled for his job) so she could show him and tell him all about it. And my mom—who pretty much thought Arnie was the only male worth anything ever since Dad left us when I was eight and then came back for a bit when I was ten, which is when the twins were born, and then left again and a couple years later ran off the road one night after leaving Supples Tavern—Mom was even smiling. And we were dressed up, Arnie and me, nothing too fancy, but Arnie wore a navy blue coat and tie, the one he wore for debate team, and I had on a long purple velveteen skirt and a lavender blouse that in the right light you could see through to my white camisole. Which was the style. We took a pass on corsages, because it wasn't really a date, but still, we both were excited (I was at least) and even though the weather had gone insane, rain and more rain, and lightning, thunder, and wind, I knew as we ran out to Arnie's VW that this was going to be some night. And back at the house, the moms were in the window, and the twins were there, too, and they were all waving. We pulled away from the curb and the wind battered against the car and the branches of the trees all bent low like they, too, were waving us on our way.

It was pretty in the gym, streamers and balloons, everybody all dressed up, and especially the lights, which were covered up with colored film. And the smell of perfume and hairspray and flowers nearly hid the smell of wet sneakers. And the music was good. I was glad that they had decided against the band, Derek Jerabek's older brother's one, the Hendrix Connection—you can guess what they played—since his brother had been sent over to Vietnam and they still didn't have a lead guitar. So they hired a disc jockey and he played records we all heard every day, the sort of thing we all would dance to in the privacy of our own homes.

Arnie and I loved to dance; we danced all the time at my house. We got right on the dance floor with everyone else, all of our long dresses sweeping over the floor, the boys undoing their ties, hands, arms, legs everywhere. And we all kept moving like we had something to prove, like if we stopped, something might catch up to us. And we danced until we were drenched and the disc jockey put on something slow. Someone turned down the lights even more, and everyone pulled together, pushed their bodies tight against each other, two by two, and pretty much just stood in the middle of the floor, shifting foot to foot, not really moving. There was a lot of kissing going on out there, and every now and again you could see one or the other of the girls pulling her head back and looking up, her face all powdery and glowing in the light, looking like she was surrounded by some sort of haze. I kept waiting for Mr. Harvey, the principal, or one of the teachers to step in, but they didn't. And from where Arnie and I stood on the side, drinking pink punch in silver paper cups, I watched all the making out and body pressing and felt something stir in me. So I tried to look past it all, and there were the teachers and Mr. Harvey, in a huddle, talking and appearing, I don't know, worried.

And then the lights went out. Just like that. And then there was a big crash, a heavy thunderclap that was so loud and close it shook the punch in my cup. And through the gym's high narrow windows, we could see the lightning flash over and over. The panes rattled. A couple of the girls, the more dramatic ones, screamed.

"Young people," Mr. Harvey yelled over the crowd, "Young people!" He always called us that. The rest of the teachers called us kids. "Listen," he yelled, and then there were a couple of flashlights shining on him; Mr. Granger, the wrestling coach had one, and Miss Daniels, the librarian had another. Mr. Harvey put a hand up to shade his eyes. "We have a bit of a problem here," he said.

"Duh," someone yelled from the center of the room. It sounded like Derek. It probably was. But no one laughed.

"Seriously," Mr. Harvey went on. "We have been informed that a funnel cloud has just touched down in Shelby. We are under a tornado warning."

Things went quietly wild then. Everyone talking and spinning around, some of the girls started crying and the boys, trying to be brave, talked in steady voices and held their dates' hands.

Mr. Harvey spoke again, "I'm sorry to say this, but prom is now officially cancelled." And people made noise like they were disappointed, like they had forgotten that just a minute ago someone had told them that a tornado was on the way. "Young people, please. If I might have your attention."

Arnie put his arm over my shoulder then. "You're shaking," he said. I tucked tight into him.

"We will now proceed, in an orderly fashion, to the basement." We'd had enough tornado drills to know better, we lived in what people called a tornado alley, and most of us had seen the funnel clouds each summer out over the flat fields, but still, when Mr. Harvey said the word "basement," kids piled into the doorway of the gym, ran down the hall, and crashed together into the stairwell. The generator had kicked in; two spotlights lit the way from a corner near the ceiling. Mr. Harvey and the teachers chased after the kids. "People! Kids! People!" they yelled. Arnie held me tightly, which helped my first instinct—to jump into the crush of kids—ease up some, and we walked quickly after the crowd. Mr. Harvey turned toward us. "Come along, you two," he said, but then he saw it was Arnie, brilliant Arnie, and me, who he knew by name only because I was never any trouble, really, or anything special either for that matter, and he just nodded and trotted toward the stairwell where everyone else was pushing and yelling.

Just when we were about to get to the stairs, Arnie stopped me. He looked into my face. "You okay?" he asked. And, you know, I really was. We could hear the noise below us in the basement, and we could hear the wind making its chugging sound outside. "Some special night, huh?" Arnie said. And he was smiling, and it was that loopy smile, like his skitching smile. And I don't know why, but I stood on my toes and pushed my breasts against his chest and put my arms around his neck and kissed him, tongue and all. And his arms went around my waist and he pulled me closer, and I could feel his hard on, right through his pants, through the velvet of my skirt. And I rubbed a little against it, felt it move over my belly, and the rain hit the windows like handfuls of pebbles. Arnie let go of my waist and took my hand and pulled me into the boys' locker room, which had a spotlight shining over the door that made the place full of shadows and dark patches. He led me along one wall and into the shower room. "Here," he said, and his voice sounded hollow and echo-y. "Sit down." He put his jacket on the floor and I sat down. And then Arnie was beside me, and we sat still and quiet, listening to the battering of things outside, to the wind, to the thunder, imagining what made what sound—was that a lamp-post? A car? The rooftop? And I started to shake again. Arnie put his arms around me.

"We could die," he said, matter-of-factly. And of course, I'd been thinking exactly that, so I just nodded. "My poor mom," he said. And I imagined Arnie's mom in their house in the dark by herself, nervous and flighty like she gets, her hands butterflies she can't keep still. And then I hoped she was at my house with my mom, who, in a case like this, an emergency situation, would know just what to do, would take all of them down to the cellar, the twins, King, Mrs. Lawlor, and they'd be down on the lino-leum floor, leaning against the dryer, the washing machine, and Mom would get their minds off things, singing something, James Taylor, maybe, or old Beatles.

"My poor mom," Arnie said again. And then, "I got my notice."

And try as I might, I couldn't figure out what he was talking about. I didn't want to sound stupid, though, in these maybe last few minutes of our life, so I didn't say anything.

"A few weeks ago. I thought I'd get a student deferment," he went on. "But they've changed the rules."

And then, even though it was hot in the shower room, I started to get cold. I knew what Arnie was telling me. Notice. Of the draft.

"I go for my physical next week," he said.

Arnie and I hardly ever talked about the war, but I knew that he had very specific ideas about it, like he had about a lot of things. Whenever someone we knew—like Derek's brother—enlisted or got drafted, Arnie would go into this mood that was part sad, part angry. And I knew when he got like that, quiet and steaming, it was best not to talk to him. At all. So that night we just sat there saying nothing, sat and listened to the tornado hit town. Waiting.

And then Arnie stretched out on the floor, and I kept sitting there listening past the wind for what I don't know. But what I heard after a while came from up close. And it was Arnie crying, which was very unlike him. The only time I heard him cry before was after Derek and Sky got me in the stacks and later, after Arnie and I kissed and everything and he went to the kitchen for the Pepsi, I heard him in there, crying like this, soft and really, really sad.

So I lay down next to him, put my head on his chest. Shushed him. But that didn't help at all, the opposite in fact. Because then the crying really started, and his body shook, and I held on, my arms tight around his waist and his crying ran through me, and I couldn't help it, I started to cry, too, but I knew that I was crying not just about Arnie, about Arnie going away, to war maybe, but about everything, everything that had ever happened before in my life that had hurt me: the way Dad came into my room that first night when he said he had to leave, the way he didn't tell me the next time he left, the way Mom's face crumpled into itself when she told me about his crash, the way the twins came home with Mom from the hospital and Dad was already gone, months gone, and the Goddamned twins with their bald heads and red, flabby faces, looked exactly like Dad did in the mornings when he was hung over. I cried about Derek and Sky feeling me up in the library, I cried about Mom going quiet for those months after the twins were born, staying in her bedroom, leaving me and Mrs. Lawlor to take care of the babies, of the house. I cried about not knowing what was going on outside while we were there in the shower room, I cried about not knowing what we'd find when we went outside, about what might be lost. I cried about not knowing—let's face it—anything at all.

We pressed together, Arnie and I, and the kissing started again, and we kept at it, good and long. Then I took off Arnie's glasses, unbuttoned his shirt, lifted his tie over his head. I pulled my own blouse out of the waistband of the purple skirt, and pulled it up over my head. But here's the thing. There we were, on our way to naked, and all the rest that goes with that, but instead of going forward, you know, going all the way, this is where we stopped. And I think maybe if we'd been two other people, like Derek and one of the other girls, we might have— probably would have—kept going. But let's face it, we were just Arnie and me. So instead he wrapped me up in his arms, pulled my head under his chin. And we stayed like that on the floor. And at first we started to tell little stories, you know, "remember when" and all. But then we stopped even that, stopped talking and just lay there, while the town took on the storm, while the world outside reeled.

There had been no siren, no sound at all that warned us about the coming of the tornado. What there was later, though, was a ringing of all the church bells in town to let everyone know it was over. In my sleep I heard them in my dreams, loud and low, but I can't remember what I dreamed. Arnie stirred under me, and we pulled apart and rearranged our clothes. We heard the drumming of feet in the hallway, everyone else running up from the basement, running toward whatever was going on out there.

Months later, after the town had cleaned up the mess left behind, cleared the trees out of the streets, hauled away the overturned cars, put up new roofs, rebuilt Jack's Super, Mrs. Lawlor turned up on our doorstep and fell into a heap before Mom could even get her to say what the army had told her. I was home from college for spring break, working part time at Jack's. I stood in the doorway, and in the pale, white spring light, I watched Mom go to Arnie's mother, watched her sink to the concrete and wrap her arms around her friend, watched her hold her. And my knees gave a bit under the weight of it all, but I reached for the doorknob and held on as best I could, and for some reason I thought about that ball Arnie threw over the fence that day when we were mowing the lawn. And I wondered where exactly it ended up once it stopped rolling.

"We didn't die," I had said to Arnie on prom night before we left the shower room. Arnie just looked at me, his lips turning up at the corners, but it wasn't a smile. Not really. Still, he nodded, I remember, and bent down to kiss me, his aim off, and he brushed my jaw with his lips.

"After you," Arnie said when we got to the locker room door. And I stepped around him into the empty hallway. We walked hand-in-hand toward the wide exit doors, and I pushed hard on the heavy silver bar that released the latch.

"After you," I said. And Arnie ran his hands over his jacket like he was smoothing it; he straightened the knot in his tie.

I stood by and held the door for him, and my best friend walked right past me, just like that, leading the way out and into the wet, wrecked night.

THE JOKE

"So you don't mind a little dirty joke, huh?"

I shook my head. What'd he think I was, some kid? Fifteen and out there way after dark—on my own I could've been. So when the old guy with the tiny scrubbed hands, small as a boy's, only veiny and bluish, offered me a lift, I thought, *sure, a place to sit for a while*. "Nice ride," I said. This big polished four-door with the seats wrapped in plastic that smelled like adhesive tape, like a family car.

He tapped his nails, white moon slivers, on the steering wheel, switched off the engine and began to speak real low, his head tilted toward mine. I had to lean in to hear him, had to strain to listen as he spoke just above a whisper about a stream of things like women getting their clothes ripped off by accident, and men accidentally putting their cocks where they didn't belong and hookers and blow jobs and butt fucks. I sort of laughed now and then, I wasn't getting it, but I acted like I did. You know. And by the time I got that it wasn't a joke, it was just dirty, it was too late because I was already there, already said I didn't mind,

I would listen. And I didn't know how to stop listening, how to get him to shut up for chrissakes, shut up, shut the fuck up, and the smell of that car, that plastic, that awful thick glue smell made my stomach churn and my eyes smart, and I couldn't turn away when he reached down and pulled his zipper, pulled his dick out, the small wrinkled gray thing that he yanked on until it bloated up too big and purple for his little boy hands, clublike and purple, larger than it should have been he was such a little guy—I could take him, he was so little—and when he whispered he wanted me to touch it, what else could I do? I was already there, already said I didn't mind, already laughed, damnit—so he took one of my hands and put it around the thick pole which was sticky and felt squirmy and loose, and he groaned and said Show me your tits, and I figured what the hell. We'd come this far, not like I could say No, I don't want to do this, because I'd already started doing it and what could I do to stop this from moving forward now, stop it and make it go back? And besides, it was better to use my hands to lift my shirt than to touch him, thank God I'd worn a bra, that was all he'd get to see. But when I pulled up the tank top it was like I was peeling my own skin, it hurt damnit, it hurt for no reason I could figure out. So I yanked it up fast like you strip off a Band-Aid, and with the shirt in front of my face at least I didn't have to see him, to see *it* for a while. And behind the shirt I felt my eyes burn and fill, felt the tears roll down my face, but no sound, not from me. And then I asked him not to touch me, whispered it quiet like a prayer, but it didn't matter what I said, he didn't care, didn't want to touch me because he was touching himself and moaning and coming into his own dry hands and I pulled down my shirt just in time to see the thing jerk and squirt and I reached behind myself for the door handle and nearly fell out of the car but caught my footing in time to back away, step away from the car which he started and took off in, wheels spitting gravel, leaving me at the side of the road. Crying and—that son of a bitch—alone all over again.

RUNNING

The race was Hoof's idea. Sunday morning, all hungover after another Saturday night at the Inn with Annie and Jim and they're both—Jackie and Hoof—moaning about needing to run.

"Why don't we ever run together," Jackie asks for maybe the hundredth time since they'd moved out to the country. In the city they'd run along the lakefront, stop at a stand on the beach, share a soda or a big bottle of water. Then they'd walk back to the apartment, hand in hand, fingers sticky from the sweat that runs down your arms in Chicago summer humidity.

"You run too slow," Hoof says.

"I can keep up," Jackie says. "Especially if you run more than your usual mile."

"I like my mile. Short and quick," he says.

It's a point of contention between them, and they both know they're not talking about the running. It's a long-haul thing; Hoof's not a long-haul sort of guy. They'd reached a time in their lives when they're supposed to be settled, more or less, but since they'd been together these past eight years, Hoof's had three jobs, gone back to and then quit graduate school, moved in with Jackie then broke up with her, and then married her, got that substantial inheritance from his father and decided to build them a nice big house in the country where they could do whatever they wanted. Not work he meant, retire early, kind of. Jackie, write like she always wanted, and Hoof, well, whatever took his attention: computers, woodworking, gardening, collecting things. The one great room of the cabin (it never got bigger than two rooms) was filled with his projects. First it was just the coffee table, then the desk that was supposed to be Jackie's, the chairs, and on this morning they had to push a dozen catalogues and a bushel of tomatoes out of the way in order to set their coffee cups down on the dining table.

They haven't made love in months.

"Come on Hoof," Jackie says.

His real name is Arnold. Arnold Huffner. But Arnold is a nerd's name, a boy with too-thick glasses and a pocket protector, a studious, plodding achiever in the fifth grade. Chess club, maybe. In high school they called him Huffer, because of the dope, he says. Because of the asthma, says his mother. But now it's Hoof. Hoof is better. He is yellow-haired and tan, broad shouldered, a brilliant smile and a look in his sleepy brown eyes that makes it hard for Jackie to not want to forgive him for not finishing things: the dishes, an argument, the cabin.

"Come on," she says again. "Let's do it my way for once."

She's whining, which she knows Hoof hates. It's what his mother used to do to wheedle him into things—take her grocery shopping, mow the lawn, call his dad for more cash. Still, whining works with Hoof.

"All right, damnit," he says. "We'll run together."

He's holding his head like it hurts. It should. They were at the Inn until closing, Annie, Jim, Hoof, and Jackie, and sometime along the line Jim suggested shots of tequila, but Annie and

Jackie kept on with their Diet Dr. Pepper and rums. Hoof got to the drunk place he gets nearly every Saturday these days, where his eyes start to slip around, find a spot and slide off, and Jim got quiet like he does while Annie starts to pick on him. It's like he's got it coming, the way he takes it from her ("Jim you're drunk," "Jim you're embarrassing me," "Jim just look at you.") and sometimes Jackie has to excuse herself from the smoky bar made tight by Annie's sniping and step out into the wide-open emptiness of midnight Main Street to keep from screaming.

She wonders what it's like to live with someone who is at you all the time. The sound of the disapproval must be deafening. In Jackie and Hoof's house, it's mostly quiet which, when you think about it, has a deafening quality of its own. Hoof hardly talks anymore; his quiet fills the two rooms. Except when he has an attack. The noise then is gruesome, his breath raggedy and gurgling, like what drowning must sound like. He never had an attack in the city, at least not that Jackie witnessed, so the first time she heard him gasping like that she ran to his side, tried to help. She didn't know what to do, pat his back, call 911, so she circled the couch, closing in on him like his body seemed to be doing, watched while he sucked on his inhaler and batted her hands away. His mouth opened and opened, and his eyes went wild and wet and filled with something. It wasn't fear, although Jackie was scared as shit. His eyes pushed at her, like if she couldn't help, then she should get out of his way. Like her being there, seeing this, wasn't at all what he needed, it could only make things worse. Jackie finally understood and left him to fend for himself. And now whenever it happens, she waits it out in the small bedroom, listens to the fight he puts up, ignores the claustrophobia blanketing her, the effect of no breath, of no escape.

This morning, neither of them is in running condition, so they take their time, move slowly through coffee and water and vitamins and cool showers and changing into running clothes. When Jackie's ready, she leaves the confines of the cabin to find Hoof on the broad steps of the porch, still holding his head.

"Ready," she says.

"I'm not sure," he says.

"Aw, Hoof, come on. You said."

"All right," he says, a sharp whisper with an edge to it, and Jackie considers backing down, giving him a break, but then he comes up with the idea.

"Let's race," he says. And he's smiling a hard smile, and his sleepy eyes are marbles now and he's pushing her again. She can tell.

"Sure," she says, and shrugs like it's no big deal. "Let's race."

Only he'd slaughter her in a race, and she knows this is also his idea. He'll give in to the running together in order to prove how even though he's got asthma, she still can't keep up, how he would have to ratchet his workout way, way down in order to do it Jackie's way. She runs slowly but she runs long, too. Five miles, six sometimes. Anyone can run fast for a mile, she thinks, but she's pretty sure that she wouldn't be able to keep up with Hoof for even that.

"You'll have to run farther, though," Jackie says.

And together they figure out a course to follow, a path of seven-plus miles that seems to make it fair: longer than Jackie would run, so she'll have to slow way down, much longer than Hoof does, so he can stop and go, run it in sprints.

"What's at stake?" She asks.

"Good question," Hoof says, and his smile is hard again.

And they're ready to run.

The hangover takes some getting beyond, but Jackie works her way through it as her legs find their rhythm and she watches the familiar pass of dirt and gravel under her feet. She breathes in the warm, expansive, green-smelling air, breathes out the tight headache from last night's binge. This is the thing she likes best about their move, this daily run. The world seems somehow bigger out here, opening in all directions. The way the land slopes and swells, the way part of the path edges a stream, part of it curves around the little lake (an Indian name meaning Water Lingers) and the bigger one (Water Lingers Still), and she even likes the straight shot of highway, a strip of gray that just goes, and goes, and goes. And this is what Jackie wants to share with Hoof, the reason why she longs for them to run together. She'd show him things; they'd talk about things. "See the blue house there?" she'd say, "It looks like sky in the trees. And look, the trailer with the sign out front: Clothes, $1 a bag. Is that buying or selling?" Some days Jackie wants it to be buying. Some days it would be better to sell. She'd show Hoof the crosses on opposite sides of the road, always freshly white with painted red numbers, 1971, 1967, and plastic wreathes. They'd make up stories about all the country people. Like they used to do in the city. Since they moved out here, Jackie's figured out that it isn't the writing she wants, it's the stories. In the city, each day they'd come home from work and talk about things. The job, the people they met, the oddballs on the subway.

Jackie passes the newer subdivision where Annie and Jim live, six styles of house in four different colors, coordinated street signs and mailboxes all built behind a curving stone gate. SuburbLand, she calls it. Anywhere, USA.

Ahead is where she'd turn if this were her usual run, where the logging road circles back to the cabin Hoof built. But the race path they decided on goes on another half-mile down to the county road. When she'd hit the highway, Hoof was already a dot way out front, but he's long gone now, running hard and uneven. Jackie imagines his body working to make more room for more air, shifting side to side like it does when he gets a momentum going. The one time they'd canoed on Water Lingers, he wanted to pick up the pace in a way the quiet little lake couldn't afford, and Jackie held onto the boat's sides as Hoof paddled right side, left side, leaning and leaning until the rig capsized and they went down and came up sputtering. Paddles, canoe, picnic basket, and beer cans bobbing on the shattered surface around them. And she nearly drowned from the laughing and Hoof, who said he was good at this sort of thing, looked pissed.

Just off the county road is a small trail that leads down to the big lake's side. Jackie nearly misses it, but then it's there, overgrown and golden in the first days of fall. And the lake is there, too, the trail opening up on its vastness, the cool of the water filling the air. And there, too, is Hoof, on his knees and throwing up, one hand in the water. And Jackie stops on the trail, yards away and behind tall grasses, unsure what to do next. She can see it's not an attack but the hangover, and Hoof sits back on his heels and wipes his mouth. She's close enough to hear the noise of his sickness and the aching sound of his moaning.

When his father died Hoof told Jackie about it over the phone. "I hardly knew him," he said, and she believed him when he said it didn't really matter. But later that night, on the balcony of their apartment in the city they looked out over the lights to the black void that was Lake Michigan, and Hoof told her about the time his father asked to see him. Hoof was just out of college then, about to start his first job, and his dad invited him to dinner. Hoof spent three and a half hours on a train that took him out of the city and past cornfields to the town his father had settled in after the divorce. "He had a gift for me," Hoof said. At the station, Hoof's father met him in an old sedan and took him to a Denny's. "A Denny's," Hoof said, and laughed, popped open another beer and leaned back in his chair, looked up the ladder of lit and unlit windows of the high-rise across the street. Hoof kept waiting for his dad to say something about the present, about Hoof's graduation, but all the old man talked about was a bridge. "We could see it from the restaurant," Hoof told Jackie. "It was this green thing, like the metal had turned. No big deal, just your average bridge. 'I made that bridge,' Dad said after a while, 'I built it.' And he was smiling. Proud. And like I said, it was just your average bridge. 'Yeah?' I said. And he kept looking at me, like he wanted me to say something else. Nodding. 'Yeah?' I said again. And then our food came. And we ate mostly in silence, passing the ketchup and Tabasco back and forth. Salt and pepper. We dressed our burgers exactly the same. And every once in a while I'd catch Dad looking out at the bridge and sometimes I thought I could see him watching me, but then I'd look up, and there he was staring at the bridge. That damn bridge. After that we had some ice cream because it came with the meal and then Dad took me back to the station where I'd get the train back to the city and before he got back in his car he shook my hand and handed me an envelope and I put it in my pocket and it wasn't until I was half-way home that I thought to even look inside. No note or anything. Five thousand bucks, though. In hundreds. But no note."

And when Hoof got to the end of the story, maybe the last one he ever told Jackie, she thought he might be crying. He wouldn't look at her. His voice was rough but his eyes, she could see in the nightlight of the city, were dry. Jackie moved her chair closer to his, but he stood up and cleared his throat and went inside to the bathroom. She stayed where she was and listened. On the balcony, though, the only noise came from the planes high over head and some drunks below, rolling bottles on the sidewalk and laughing. And then Hoof went straight to bed without even saying good night, and the next day, and maybe the next, too, he didn't talk to Jackie at all.

He's still on his knees lakeside and Jackie doesn't want him to get mean like he does when she sees him like this, weak, so she backs down the trail as quietly as possible and turns to run. She moves blindly at first, trying to outrun the closing-in feeling, to put as much land between Hoof and herself as possible. And she's not entirely surprised when sometime later she looks up and around and realizes she has absolutely no idea where she is. The trees look taller here, and the trail gives way to prairie grasses and grasshoppers. She could turn around, but she doesn't want to go backwards this time. Jackie wants to move on, even if she doesn't know exactly what that means. And she skips over the weeds and insects and nothing looks familiar and after two years in the two rooms of the cabin with silent Hoof, she can't help but feel good about this. When was the last time she was lost? Her legs feel light on the uneven land, and her headache is gone. Jackie runs and runs and runs. There's nothing to stop her.

When they first got out to the country, Jackie wanted Hoof to read her stories. She wanted him to talk about them with her. But when he finished something he'd just nod and set it aside. "Good," he'd say if she asked. Or, "Fine." It wasn't enough. Jackie didn't care if he liked them, really, that wasn't what it was about. She just wanted something to start them off, to get things going again like coming home to each other from work did back in the city. So Jackie started to write stories about other men. She made them all up, they both knew that, but she gave them to him one after another and watched him read silently, watched that pulse move just under his temple like he was chewing on something hard. The stories weren't any good, even Jackie knew that, but something must have been working in them because by the time he finished, Hoof looked nothing but angry. And the next one she gave him would be worse than the last, the woman more Jackie, the man less Hoof, and she kept hoping he'd say something maybe, even tell her to stop. But he didn't. And after a while when she gave them to him he'd just put the pages down and pick up a catalogue or a book or his beer. "Hoof," she'd say. "I'll get to it," he'd say. Only he didn't. Hoof stopped reading them and so there was no good reason for Jackie to write them.

She's out there in the fields and woods she doesn't know for a long time, and after a bit Jackie stops thinking about all the things she thought she knew for certain (the day of the week, the bratwurst Hoof will cook on the grill, the twelve pack of beer Annie and Jim will bring to dinner, the way Annie will glower at Jim who will look at her like he didn't mean it, whatever he's done this time, the way Hoof won't look at Jackie no matter what she says unless he feels he's being challenged, the way the evening will slip into night and they will all drink too much and when they climb into bed, Hoof will put his back to Jackie) and think about what she has yet to find out. How she can find her way back to the cabin. How she can keep on running if she wants. How the land opens up beyond that next stand of trees. How Hoof will or won't cry when she tells him she's leaving.

It's funny how you see some things so clearly in certain moments of your life. The land did open up just past that stand of trees like Jackie thought it would. And the sun was bright there, yellow and so harsh it made her eyes sting. But just past that is where SuburbLand was built, and then the sight of what she knew made Jackie feel bad and good at the same time. She walked down the close and planned streets of the subdivision, and up to Jim and Annie's door. She looked through the little diamond of glass and saw the two of them watching TV on the couch, Jim's head in Annie's lap, Annie's hand in Jim's hair. And instead of knocking, Jackie turned around and ran back home along the familiar path.

And there at the cabin sat Hoof on the porch, his shirt off, his chest gleaming and wet, the waistband of his shorts dark with sweat. He held out a jug of water, and pulled Jackie onto his lap. They sat there and no matter what, she couldn't bring herself to say anything, but then Hoof did. He told her about this deer he came across in the woods.

"Near the lake," he said. "It was little and still had its spots, I almost didn't see her. She was down in the brush."

Jackie nodded him on, felt the damp silk of his hair against her temple.

"I was wishing you were there to see it; I couldn't believe she was letting me get so close. I kept expecting her to jump up, run away. I thought, Goddamn! This is really something, me and her. Only..."

And Jackie waited, like she'd learned to wait over these last years, for Hoof to either finish or just give up.

"Only when I got right over her, she was dead. It didn't matter how close I got, she was already gone. A hole the size of a quarter under her ear. Her eyes were open, big and bright. Only there were flies. Lots and lots of flies."

He took a long swallow of water, cool condensation dripped onto Jackie's thigh.

"Kids, probably. Kids," Hoof said. "Where were you?" He said, "I didn't know where you were."

"Me either," Jackie said. She thought of Hoof on his knees next to the lake, moaning.

"Lost, I guess," she said.

They went back into the cabin Hoof built and they showered together and made love before Jim and Annie pulled up the gravel drive.

"You win," Jackie told Hoof while they were still on the bed. He nodded. "What do you want?" Jackie asked.

"What do you want?" Hoof asked.

He held her gaze like he could, his eyes wide enough to let Jackie in. And she thought of what she'd meant to say, what she had decided on the trail.

"A new house," Jackie said finally.

Hoof nodded.

"Sure," he said. "I'll build it."

Before Jackie could reply, Hoof shifted beside her, gathered her up and tucked himself around her. And under the familiar weight of his muscled arm Jackie imagined how it must be for him when the air doesn't come. Even though you can't really see it, you know it's there, right there, all around you. Somehow, you just need to get it. And so you open your mouth and try over and over, but still you just can't do it. It's like this: no matter what you do, no matter how hard you try, you just can't get what you need.

WHEN IS A DOOR NOT A DOOR?

I just supposed it would be a little kid. You know, *baby* sitting? So you can imagine my surprise when the mom opened the door and there was this, well, *young lady* in the shadows behind her.

"Good morning," said Mrs. Emory. She was my mom's boss. My mom got me the job—said it would do me good, said I needed structure. Want to know what I think? This structure thing was more for her than it was for me. Something she needed because of Danny (my brother) and all. Anyway. "Emily," Mrs. Emory said, and crooked her arm around the waist of her daughter to pull her forward, "This is Christy. Christy, Emily."

Emily Emory? Poor kid.

Emily looked me up and down, her wide almond-shaped eyes waggling in her round, flat face. I gave a little wave. "Hi," I said.

"Hi," Emily said. She was at least two inches taller than me (I'm littler than most my age) and probably outweighed me, too.

"Hi," I said again, standing like a dope on the front step, shifting from one foot to the other.

"Hi," Emily said. Her mom smiled at her like she'd just done something wonderful.

I laughed and said "Hi," again, but Emily repeated it solemn as shit and I immediately felt a little sorry I'd started this.

"Well," Mrs. Emory said, and moved to the side enough for me to come in finally. She held her hand out in a sweeping motion, hostess style, and Emily did the same. Only I don't think Emily was joking, and it kind of gave me the creeps.

The living room was like something I'd seen on television, *The Avengers* maybe, or *Love American Style*. Brass and glass everything. Big, soft leather couches the color of caramel, and butterscotch shag carpet about two inches long. These people had a bundle. Mrs. Emory dressed like a boss. She wore a skirt and a blouse that I'm pretty positive was silk. It was one of those multicolored things, something meant to look cool and young, but mostly just looked expensive. She wore her hair short and no-nonsense, all streaked up and sprayed in place. She was old, I couldn't help but notice. Lines stretched across her forehead and in rays around her mouth, and her eyes had a sort of milkiness to them that reminded me of my grandmother. Not that she was that old. But still, Mrs. Emory was pushing fifty, I'd bet, and that made me wonder about Emily.

"How old are you?" I asked Emily as we sat down across from one another in the leather couches. Emily looked at her mom. Mrs. Emory nodded.

"Twelve."

I tried to keep the surprise off my face. This kid was big for twelve. Tall and, well, *developed*. She had these big boobs that were beginning to hang down toward her stomach, and judging from the way her blouse sort of flattened over them, they were not yet holstered by any sort of bra—training or otherwise. And boy, could she have used one.

"How old are you, Christy?" Mrs. Emory asked. Nice as pie, but still I sensed she might have been as freaked as I was at how much bigger Emily was than me, and I can't say why for sure, but that irked me.

"Fifteen," I said and sat up straight. I pushed my chest out some. I had a pretty good set of boobs myself. "Going on sixteen. I'll be a junior."

Mrs. Emory gave me one of those fakey kindergarten teacher grins. "So your mother says." She was still standing in the middle of the room, and I sort of wished she'd either sit down or I hadn't, but there wasn't much I could do about that.

"What grade are you in, Emily?" I asked.

Mrs. Emory put a hand on her daughter's shoulder. Emily looked up at her and then back at me, her wide eyes blinking. "Oh, Emily's not in a grade, really. She's at a special school." And the way Mrs. Emory said it, low and whispery, it was like she was revealing some huge secret. And then I began to get what was going on here, like all of a sudden it got through to me. Emily was—what was the word my mom said about these kinds of kids?—*slow*.

"That's nice, huh?" I said, and my voice got louder, I could tell, and that was stupid because Emily was just slow, not deaf. Still, it was like I couldn't help it. My words just kept on going that way, loud and disconnected. "Special school?" I looked straight at Emily, she stared back flatly. "Do…you…like…it?" Emily just shrugged. Mrs. Emory's smile stretched a little tight across her teeth.

"Well," she said and patted Emily on the shoulder. "I suppose I should be heading out." But she just stood there, making no move to head out whatsoever. "You girls will get along fine, I'm sure," she kept up the tight smile, but her eyes looked worried. I nodded up and down emphatically.

"We'll be fine. You bet." And I stood up and took a step to where Emily sat all hunched up on the opposite couch. She leaned back with her whole body to look up at me. I put my hand out in her direction but she just pushed back against the cushions and moved her eyes side to side from me to her mom. I worked to keep my voice normal, not too loud, not too slow. Normal. "Emily? Whaddaya think, huh? We'll be fine?" Emily shrugged and laced her fingers in that way they teach you in school and then turned her hands over to show the flat plane of her palms.

"People?" She asked and looked up at her mom who I'm pretty sure by now was rethinking this whole babysitting bit. And I'll tell you, that made me sort of steamed. Not like I couldn't handle some twelve-year-old kid. Some twelve-year-old slow kid, for chrissakes.

I sat down on the couch next to Emily, scooted over as close as she would allow me to. Close enough that I could smell her, something like cooked carrots and baby powder and sweaty armpits. "Here," I said and made my hands into the church, fingers tucked down between the knuckles. Emily repeated my moves. Mrs. Emory did it, too. "Here's the church," I said, and then made a point with my index fingers. Mom and daughter did the same. "Here's the steeple," I said and then turned my hands over slowly. "Open the doors and see all the—"

"People!" Emily said in a booming voice. Mrs. Emory dropped her own church and clapped for us both.

"Yes!" She said and smiled for real this time. "Good job, Emily. Good job, Christy." And you ask me, she was going a little overboard here, you know, gushing. "Oh, yes! You two will get along just great!"

And then she took me on a tour of the house while Emily played the hands game over and over and over again, her voice sing-songy with the rhymes.

"Thanks so much for taking time off from your summer vacation," Mrs. Emory said as she yanked open the double-wide refrigerator to reveal shelves of Pepsis and Hawaiian Punch and shiny red apples and Tupperware fitted into perfect little stacks with pink, blue and green covers. "I really, really appreciate it. I wasn't sure what I'd do without a sitter, especially since her last one...." And Mrs. Emory's face went dark in a flash, and sort of mean, really, too, but then just as quick it cleared and she put on what I guessed was one of her boss smiles, you know, shiny and sincere-looking and all. Then she said, "Well, you know what they say—when one door closes...." I nodded, but I had no idea what she was talking about. Mrs. Emory reached for a small plastic square, a sandwich holder I think, and an apple. She turned to look at me, and I couldn't help but notice under her perfect hair that one of her eyebrows was just a smidgen shorter than the other. "Anyway, thanks again, Christy, really. I mean it. Really." I nodded and waved it off like it was no big deal, but you know, it really was.

We went back into the living room where Emily was still playing church-steeple-people and Mrs. Emory gave the big girl a kiss on the top of her head. "See you later, sweetie pie, okay?" She said. Emily gave her mother a blank look and shrugged before she turned her attention back to her hands.

At the door Mrs. Emory said, "Thanks again, Christy, dear." I hate it when someone you don't even know calls you dear. Unless it's a cute guy or something. We shook hands and I started to push the door closed between us when Mrs. Emory grabbed my hand in hers again. "And Christy? Dear?"

I made myself smile. "Yes? Ma'am?"

"I'm sorry about your brother," she said and held onto me. I looked at the mat beneath her feet. *Emory* swirled in silver cursive over a background of royal blue and a yellow so bright it made my eyes smart. I blinked and nodded, not willing to look up. "I mean," she said, and then stopped. "Well, anyway. I'm sorry."

"Yeah," I said and shook off her grip.

Man, why'd she have to go and say that?

I'm not sure how the news came, but I picture the words in little dark lines on the slip of a telegram. Something like "We regret to inform you" and "missing in action" I'm thinking. All I know for sure is that when I got home from school that day two weeks ago, the last day of classes, Mom's car was already in the driveway. It scared me, her car there like it never was before five, and I ran all the way from the corner to our front door. There Mom was waiting for me, just standing in the foyer, arms at her sides. And when I came in, she tilted my head back and looked into my eyes. "Cee," she whispered—it's what she calls me when it's just us—and then she got this really weird face, like her features were melting. It was so—I don't know—*extreme*, that at first I thought she must be making some sort of joke. But just as I was about to smile a little, to push her hands away from my face, she slid herself all the way down my body, folded up and into herself until she came to rest in a pool at my feet. And when I got past the whole freakiness of the thing, I knelt down there next to her, and we hugged each other and even though I had no idea what was up (okay, I had an idea, you couldn't know anyone over there in that stupid war and not carry around these ideas) I started to cry and Mom was crying and we both hugged and cried and that's when she told me. And we just stayed there, down on the cold tile of the foyer, tangled up together and crying.

And since then, we hardly ever talked about it.

Emily had a roomful of toys, little kids' things, mostly, but very expensive shit. And I'd watch her in there, surrounded by all these huge stuffed animals and a pastel painted doll house big enough to sit inside and Raggedy Anns and Andys with their own wooden rockers and a whole shelf of Barbies and some electronic gizmos that made farm sounds or flashed lights or rolled around the room with the touch of a button—and she'd just sit there on her bed with its perfect pink gingham spread and fluffy pillows and she'd play church-steeple-people. I mean, where's the sense in that? It sort of got to me, only I'm not entirely sure why. I mean, I was mad, see, but I wasn't sure if I was mad about the toys or about her not playing with them or what exactly. I plopped down on the bed next to her and put my feet up on her headboard. She slid a little closer to the footboard.

"Emily," I said. I pulled a piece of Bazooka from my pocket, crumpled up the wrapper and the joke without even reading it. They were all the same. Emily fiddled with her fingers, but kept quiet and watched me while I chewed. "You know what, Emily?" I said. She shrugged. "I'm bored."

"Want to see my panties?" Emily said. I about choked.

"Excuse me?"

"Want to see my panties?" She had one of those low, precise voices, you know, hitting the t's and p's hard. Emily stood up and started to yank on the sides of her yellow cotton trousers and I could see a red line where the elastic waist band had dug into her pudgy white belly and I sat up quick and put my hands on hers.

"No, Emily."

She let go of her pants and let her arms hang loose. Her thin little eyebrows pulled all down and scrunched. "No?" She said.

"No," I said. "No. Thanks though," I added. To be polite.

"Hey, you know what let's do?" I said after maybe a million years of silence in that toy-stuffed room, "Let's go to the park. Okay? Would you like that, Emily?"

She shrugged.

Emily walked slowly past the houses that were big but pretty much the same, stopping to look at everything: a smooshed worm on the sidewalk; an old guy with a wild ring of white hair around his spotted old head coming down his driveway toward his mailbox (he paused midway and stared back at Emily like they were playing lookaway or whatever you call it, till I took her hand and kind of tugged her along); a tiny egg lying in the grass, blue and perfect except for one end that was cracked open. I couldn't blame her on that one, it was pretty cool, and we picked it up and looked into its hollow insides and then she asked could she keep it and I said sure. But when she cradled it in her hand I couldn't help but remember that time when Danny and I found a whole nest, eggs and all, under the big maple in our front yard. And Danny—being the kind of person he is, better than most—got this idea. And I stood there waiting for him to climb up the ladder and place the nest back in the tree, and I handed the eggs up one after another, gentle as can be, and the next day we found the nest on the ground again only then the eggs were all broken and empty and Danny said "Shit" for the first time and we laughed at the word even though it was really sad about the eggs.

Emily was stopped again, kicking at something I couldn't see on the sidewalk.

"Come on, damnit," and I pulled her hand and felt the weight of her body resist me before she followed. But I kept on walking. I wasn't about to look at her round, stupid, hurt eyes.

The houses around the park were the same colors (brown, mustard, beige) as the other ones in the subdivision, but were huge, big enough to hold millions of people each. And it was one of those perfect days, all sun but not too much heat, and dry. Still, with all those big houses and all that sun, the park itself was empty. I figured it must have been that everyone around here was on vacation, or maybe the kids were at camp (like all of my so-called friends were) or already grown or something. Anyway, it kind of gave me the creeps. And to top that off, Emily was sulking and didn't want to go on any of the rides or anything, even though they were some of the coolest I've seen, all done in wood and rope so they sort of blended in with the park itself. There was this set of swings like nothing I'd ever been on, old tires and rope ladders and a huge rope web stretched millions of feet between a couple of big, fat wooden stumps like a giant hammock. I was hoping maybe Emily would like to crawl around on that one, because I sort of wanted to, but she didn't. She just sat on a bench whispering "open the doors" over and over and stared hard into the blue egg, mashing it up against her eye enough so that it started to crack a little more around its opening. And I supposed I could have played on the park stuff by myself, but I was fifteen, after all, and it would be more than a little babyish. So I sat there with her, looking around and preparing myself for more boredom. I opened another piece of Bazooka, but before I could toss the comic, Emily reached for it.

"Read," she said.

"Sure." Something to do at least. "'Hey, Joe!'" I read, and Emily had her big head tipped down over the little square of drawings and I could smell the shadowy stink of her dirty hair. I went on, really working it for some reason, making voices and stuff. "'When is a door not a door?'…'I don't know, when is a door not a door?'… 'When it's ajar.'" I handed the comic over to Emily who studied the pictures for a whole minute, and then looked at me and opened her mouth and laughed one big "HA!" Then she said, "More."

So I pulled out another piece, only this time I handed the gum to her. She held it up to her nose and took a couple of big whiffs before she shoved it into her mouth, chewed once, twice, with her mouth open, and then swallowed the stuff down. "Read," she said.

"'Did you hear the Mexican weather report?'" I read from the first panel. The bright sound of ice cream bells came from around the corner. I looked across the park for the familiar white truck.

"Read," Emily said again.

"Chili today and hot tamale," I recited without looking and handed the comic over to her. She studied it same as before and then "HA!" She folded it into a tiny square and stuffed it into her fist with the other one and the egg that was more broken shell now than anything. "More," she said.

"All right," I said, "but this is my last piece. Why don't you chew it for a while this time," I suggested. But of course, Emily swallowed the gum down again, and to tell you the truth, I couldn't really blame her. I've done the same myself millions of times. The ice cream truck circled the park slowly.

"Whaddaya say, Emily? Ice cream?"

She looked at me and then at her watch, which was not real, see, but a toy one with a picture of Barbie's face and painted-on hands that pointed to the twelve and six. She shrugged.

"Yeah, it's early I know," not quite eleven, but I was hungry and in charge. "Tell you what, let's have ice cream now, and then we'll go back to your house and have peanut butter sandwiches for dessert. All right?"

That damn shrug.

I left Emily on the bench and went to wave the truck down.

"What'll it be, Smiley?"

He was the cutest guy I had ever seen in my whole, entire life. Sandy gold hair, sort of long, and these freaky eyes. Greenish, but blue, too. He wore this bright white T-shirt and these tight white jeans, and he stood behind the wide serving window with his hands reached up high and holding onto something, his whole body stretched long. Man, the sight of him made my mouth water. Really.

"Uh," I said, and stared at the thousands of pictures on the side of the truck like I hadn't seen them a million times and like I wasn't going to order the same thing I always did. "Hmm," I said.

"That your mom?" The guy asked. And I turned around startled for a second, like maybe Mom had snuck up on me like she's done more than once when I've had guys over and we're down in the rec room messing around, like how I caught her that time looking in my drawers—good thing I'd shoved the rubbers down into the toe of one of my old winter boots. But the guy was looking at Emily. And from the back, you could tell why he might've thought that, her being so womanly and sitting all hunched over like she does and wearing those yellow cotton trousers and white blouse like a mom would.

"Nah," I said, and then, don't ask me why, "She's my sister."

"Your sister?" And his eyes sort of lit up. "Older sister?" He was probably twenty, I figured, old as Danny the last time I saw him, but the way I figured it, not too old for me, so his acting that way, all interested in my older sister, sort of pissed me off.

"No," I said, "younger."

"Younger?" And he let out a low whistle, his teeth glinting just a bit between his lips. "Man," he said, "she's big."

"She's slow," I said. Like maybe that would explain it. "Okay, I know what I want."

The ice cream guy leaned way over into the cooler to get my order, and I got a good eyeful of his butt, nice and round and hard.

"Seventy cents," he said when he was upright again.

I fished three quarters out from my back pocket. "Keep the change," I said, kidding, only he nodded and winked at me.

"Thanks, Smiley." Pretty funny how he kept calling me that. The thing is, I'm really not much of a smiler, as you might imagine. Still, I put on a big one for him when he passed the ice cream to me. "Here you go. One for Smiley, and one for Smiley's sister."

"Emily," I called back to the bench. Emily got up slowly and, holding her fistful of comics and eggshell out in front of her, she walked over to us. If she had been my real sister, I think maybe I'd be embarrassed about this time, you know, feeling like the ice cream guy might wonder if whatever was wrong with Emily could be wrong with me, too. But since she wasn't my sister, and I didn't really feel embarrassed or anything, I watched for his reaction. I could see his eyes widen as she came at us, all that loose boob flesh just rolling under Emily's blouse. I tossed my hair a little and arched my back to push up my own chest and decided that tomorrow Smiley was going without a bra.

"Hi, Emily," the guy said when she got close, "I'm Sky." Great name. Perfect.

Emily dropped her chin down and stared at the ground. "She's a little shy, Sky," I said, and, "She's scared of boys."

Emily began eating the ice cream bar, taking big bites out of first one side, then the other. She stood a yard or so from us, holding one of the comics open and she mouthed different words between bites: "Hot tamale, when is a door, it's ajar, knock knock."

"She can read, it looks like," Sky said, and then he glanced at his watch and climbed back into the driver's seat.

"Gotta go," he said and ran his hand back through all that golden hair of his.

"Sure," I said.

"See you, Emily," Sky called over my head. He shifted into go gear. The truck lurched a bit. "See you—hey," he said just as he started to pull away, "what's your name, Smiley?"

"Christy," I said. And then, easy as pie, "Christy Emory." And I sort of even liked the way it sounded.

Back at the house we had peanut butter sandwiches just like I had promised, and we ate them on the leather couches. Emily hadn't liked that idea at first. "Uh uh, no eating," she'd said even as she trotted after me into the caramel and butterscotch room. "Uh huh," I'd said and laid the plates and napkins out like a picnic, popped open two sweating bottles of Pepsi. The leather squeaked under our butts, and whenever I moved Emily laughed "HA!" and said, "Excuse you!" To tell the truth, it was kind of funny at first, but it got old pretty quick. When we finished, Emily stood up and brushed her hands together and said "Nap time," which seemed like an excellent idea, and before I could even get up and clear away our things, she was down the hall and in her room and closing the door behind her.

I wandered around the house opening closets and drawers, rummaging through Mrs. Emory's thousands of silk scarves, through her nightgowns which were for the most part flannel and not at all sexy. Mr. Emory was a mystery to me. I'd never seen him, never even heard Mom talk about him. Not like she would or anything (she didn't even talk about her own husband—ex—the guy who was my father that I only knew by Christmas and birthday cards that came postmarked from Alaska) but still. So I searched around for the signs of Mr. Emory, and in the back of the closet of what I figured for his study (heavy wooden paneling, fat, leather bound books, the hugest desk I'd ever seen) I found a little safe that had been left open (what's the point?) and there were dozens of those little folders of coins, round circles cut into the pages where you could stuff a dime, nickel, half-dollar or whatever above the gold-lettered name and date label. There were coins from as far back as before the turn of the century. I flipped through until I found the year I was born, 1956, but that page was empty. Matter of fact the coins were all from before 1950 (when Danny was born) and I'd be lying if I said that didn't tick me off. Like whatever happened after that wasn't important enough to hold onto.

I sat there inside the closet in front of that stupid safe with the little book open on my lap, steaming. I wanted to do something, to make a statement, only I wasn't sure what that should be. I could've stolen some of the coins, shit, I could've stolen the whole lot of them. The only thing is, I may be a liar (and more than a few other not so great things) but one thing I never have been is a thief. So instead I searched my pockets for whatever coins I had, scanned them for the dates. There was one from 1959, but other than that they were all from the sixties. Shit. Still, I flipped back through the pages to the year Danny was born and put the shiniest quarter I had in that slot. In my year I put a nickel. And I thought about putting one in this year, 1971, to mark the news about my brother, but I decided against it. For some reason that seemed better left untouched.

At dinner that night Mom asked me how my day was. Only when I answered her, told her about Emily and her slow self and her wanting to show me her underpants and all the big bucks things the Emorys had, well, I could tell she wasn't really listening. We were having macaroni and cheese, one of the dishes I can really make well (just follow the box and add a bunch of parmesan) and Mom hadn't even bothered to put any on her plate. Instead she had a glass full of bourbon and a cigarette, and the whole time I talked, she sort of nodded and all, like she was paying attention, but her eyes were fixed on the six-inch Sony with the sound down, where the Goddamn evening news had the bad taste to be showing film from the war like it was appropriate dinner entertainment. And even though it was in black and white, it still looked horrible, sickening, bloody and evil, and it was nearly enough to make a girl lose her appetite and I couldn't figure why Mom would want to see that, but she did. She moved her face forward, pulled the little TV box by its handle even closer, nearly pressed her nose up against it. She squinted.

"Christy, look!" She said and sat back just an inch, moved her big head out of the way. She poked a finger up against the screen, and its cigarette-stained tip looked yellow and fake next to the stark black and white flat reality of some passed out bloody guy on a stretcher, one leg shy. "Is it him?" She asked, her voice tight and squeaky. The soldier was big and dark-haired, we are all small and light. "Oh God, oh God. I can't bear to look. Cee? Cee?" But she was looking the whole time, her eyes glued on the moving picture of someone else's son. "Cee? Cee?"

And it killed me to say it, but I did. "No, Mom, it's not him."

The bloody black and white picture switched to a close-up of a big, greasy plate of fried chicken, and Mom poured herself another three fingers and sat up straight and wiped her face with both hands. When she looked at me, it was like she could barely stand the sight of me. Like she hated me. "You don't know," she said so low it was hard to even hear. "It could have been him." And she might as well have spit razor blades at me; it felt just exactly like that. She lit a new cigarette off the one that was still burning. She ground the old one hard into her empty plate. "You don't know." She stared out through the sheer yellow kitchen curtains toward the driveway.

I stood up, my entire insides pushing against my skin, hard and thick like the knot you get in your throat that means you're going to cry.

"You gonna have any of this?" I asked looking down into the pot of rubbery orange noodles.

And when she didn't even bother to look at me, much less answer even a "hell no" or anything, I dumped the whole mess into the roar of the garbage disposal.

My mom was always doing things like that, trying to see things that really weren't there. Me, on the other hand, I'd try to *not* see those things that really *were* there. Like the time a couple weeks later when Sky and me were rolling around in the rope web at the park, making out like crazy (we'd tried talking the first few days, I can't even remember about what, but finally figured out we were better at this), and Emily comes back from a trip to the public john, shuffling over to us with her pants, undies and all, down around her ankles. Sky stops short, pulls his tongue out of my ear and gives a low whistle. When I see what he's looking at—Emily half-naked and so unexpectedly beautiful it makes my gut ache—at first I bury my head in his chest and try to wish the picture away, but from this angle I can see the bulge under his zipper and can hear his breath speed up and I know it's not going away. So I swing down off the web and tell him not to look while I pull Emily back together, cover up her smooth, white legs, her round, sloped hips, her silky, golden triangle. "Here, let me help," I say, and Emily tries to explain, "I got stuck." But I don't really care what happened, I just want to not see how perfect she is anymore.

And later that day I doze off in Mr. Emory's study during naptime, and I dream a little about Danny, I think, and then I wake up with Emily above me, shaking me. And her fingers are like claws in my shoulder, her face looms over mine, her eyes shining and hard as marbles. I come to pretty fast, but not fast enough, I guess, because she begins to pull me off the couch, and there's nothing I can do to stop that, her being so much bigger and stronger than me.

"Emily, man, cool it," I say and try to right myself, try to shake loose of her grip, try to sit up before I land on the floor. But she has me. And the wind's knocked out of me as I hit ground, and I lay there for a second, trying to breathe, and then she kneels on my chest—which doesn't help the breathing one bit—and starts to shake me some more, her whole face hard and mean and tight and I can't help but think how she looks like her mother. And she says something quiet, like she's trying the word out, but I think I hear it anyway: "Slut." My head begins to bounce on the floor, and I know that if she wants to, she can really, really hurt me. So my mind goes into overdrive and I pull a wrestling move Danny taught me, and then I'm on top of her and before I can even think about it, I'm slapping her, once, twice, across the face. And her mean, tight look just slides away, and it's blank-faced slow Emily down there now, only her eyes fill up, and she looks at me with such flat calmness—even as the tears run over and down the sides of her cheeks and fill her ears—that I swear I feel my heart just crack wide open, and I stand up and walk over to the window and look out onto the perfect rows of Mrs. Emory's flower garden. Only I can't see the plants, all I can see is Emily's face. Emily's round, flat, drenched face. Shit.

And then a few days later I'm outside the Emorys' house, on my way home but without my backpack, so I turn back to the front door and reach to push the bell. But before I do, I raise up on my toes and look inside the little diamond shaped window and can see into the caramel and butterscotch room, and there's my backpack on the couch and there's Emily and her mother. Only Emily's sort of slumped over, shoulders forward, and Mrs. Emory is trying to lift her daughter's chin, but Emily keeps dropping it down, tucking it into her chest. And I remember how the week before I'd tied this hand-made choker around Emily's thick neck, how when we stood next to each other and looked at our reflections in the mirror I couldn't help but see that she was nearly a head taller than me. It was like a picture out of one of her kiddy books: the small, smart human person next to the big, dumb, not quite human giant. And even as I thought that, I hated myself for it. Still, that's what I saw, and that's what I thought. But now I see Mrs. Emory use one hand to push against Emily's forehead, and the other to swipe the string of beads off the girl's neck. Beads fly everywhere, catching light before they fall, and Mrs. Emory is screaming, I can tell by her face, and I can hear some of it, "...slut...dirty...not my..." and Emily gives her that same flat, calm look she gave me that time in her father's study, and I can't see this for sure, but I'd bet she's crying. And I wish for a second that I was a better person. Because a better person would go back in there. A better person would do something. Danny would do something. And then Mrs. Emory says something else and Emily pulls down her trousers and that's when I have to leave, I have to get out of there even though there's no where for me to go but home.

And since I don't have my keys, I'm going to have to ring the bell, and I don't want to because every time the doorbell rings in our house lately, we both freeze, me and Mom, afraid of what's out there, of all those things we don't yet know. So I pace the front walk for a bit, hoping Mom will see me out here and will open the door, will be glad I didn't ring, will be glad it's me this time. But pretty soon I figure I've walked a hundred miles up and down in front of our house, so I go over to the kitchen window and look in. And there's Mom in her usual place at the kitchen table behind a full, smoking ashtray and a glass of booze, only her head is down and she is sobbing so hard her shoulders lift and lower and her whole body shakes. And I look around to see if maybe there's another one of those yellow pieces of telegram paper only there's nothing but her and the smokes and the whiskey and that damned Sony TV. And my gut feels empty and my head feels full, and I don't know why but it's like I'm looking through these super strength glasses or something. Every line is straight, every angle sharp, every color vivid as hell. And I can see everything, more than just my mom, my house, my kitchen. Everything. Like: there's Emily, sent to her room where she sits and plays church-steeple-people a few times, then takes stock of her little inventory of Bazooka comics, eggshell, ice cream sticks and a couple beads she pinched from the floor when her mother turned her back. There's Mr. Emory (even though I don't know what he looks like) in his study, smoking a pipe and flipping a corduroy slipper on the end of his big toe, leafing through his books of coins, humphing over the shiny newer quarter and nickel. There's my dad (even though I only sort of know what he looks like) in plaid flannel and work boots, chopping down a huge tree all by himself under what I figure to be the Goddamn Aurora Borealis. And there's Sky, restocking his freezers and counting out his bank, slipping a couple of bucks into the tight pocket of his white jeans like I've seen him do before when he didn't know I was watching. And finally there's Danny, far, far away and face down in a nest of weeds and sticks. And I can see—even though it'll be months and months before we find this out—I can see sure as shit that Danny is dead.

Now this is stupid, but when the doorbell rang and I looked through the window and I saw the back of that head with that sandy hair, for a second, just a second, I believed in my soul it was Danny. I flung open the door. Sky stood on the stoop, his hair streaming with rain.

"How'd you find me?" I said when I could.

Sky pointed down to the silver letters on the welcome mat. "Your name," he said. And by the time he added, "The only Emory in the book," I remembered that he thought I was Emily's sister, that he now thought I lived here in this big house. I knew better than to let him come in, but that didn't keep me from stepping aside so he could. The electricity was out from the storm, the foyer was dark. Sky gave one of his low whistles when he saw the plush living room, candles everywhere. He winked at me. "Beautiful *and* rich, babe," he said. "Anything else you're keeping from me?" I thought about everything Sky didn't know about me, which was just that—everything. I thought about how I never told him anything and how, too, he never bothered to ask.

Emily slinked around at the end of the hallway, keeping close to the wall.

"It's just Sky," I said. "You know, Sky?" And he waved and Emily turned her face away, pressed her nose up against the wall like kids sometimes do when they're shy all of a sudden. "Get us a towel?" I asked her, and she skittered past toward the bathroom, the back of her head to us.

"I figured I wasn't gonna sell a lot of ice cream in this weather," Sky said.

It had been raining all morning, no thunder or anything, just the heavy downpour. Emily had been nervous all morning, too. And scared, I could tell, she wasn't willing to let me out of her sight. The three of us sat in the living room, Sky on the big leather chair I figured was reserved for Mr. Emory, since I'd never seen Emily or her mom ever sit there and since Emily kept giving him some sort of evil eye—or at least the best she could come up with. We sucked on Pepsis in the candle glow. None of us said anything for a long time.

"Ask Emily what's the Mexican weather report," I said, finally, when the quiet got to be too much.

"Emily," Sky said, playing it up like it really was important to him, "What's the Mexican weather report?"

"Chili today and hot tamale," she said like she knew the words by heart but they were some foreign language and she had no idea what they meant.

Sky laughed, a big, loud, phony laugh and Emily slid deeper into her place on the couch, wrapped her arms around herself. Rain splattered against the windows.

"Maybe it's time for a nap, Emily," I said. She nodded a little like she does when I tell her something she wants to believe—like it's okay to have ice cream before lunch—only she's not sure I've got the proper authority. I took her arm and walked her down the hall and got her laid out on her fluffy pink bed with her comics and eggshell and ice cream sticks and beads all within reach on the pillow next to her, and went back to Sky in the living room.

Only Sky's not there. I get a little nervous, but only for a second, because his truck's still out front so I know he's not really missing.

And when I find him, it's in Mr. Emory's study and he's got this silver candle holder down on the floor with a single candle and the way he's sitting there all cross-legged and his hair spilling over his sweet, sweet face, well my breath stops up short in my chest and I have to stand in the doorway for just a bit, hold onto the doorknob until the rubber in my legs solids itself up enough for me to walk normal, to pull the door almost closed and then to ease down on the rug next to him, to let him pull me in, kiss me, unbutton my blouse, and so on. And then we're down there on old Mr. Emory's rug, you know, just where I suppose I'd been longing to be all summer and I'm thinking this is it, this is it— and of course it is because we're both pretty much naked and we're kissing and all and it feels just like it's supposed to, skin on skin. And it's raining hard now, the windows rattling and there's thunder now, too, only far, far away. And I think "flood" for some reason, just like that, the word, I mean, and then Sky turns me over, and it's like I'm floating, the way he moves me, easy as that. And as I'm turning—my face away from his, him kissing my neck, my back—I'm thinking, yes, yes, right, right. But then I notice how the closet door is open and behind that, the safe, and I can't help but hope that Sky doesn't see it, but it's like he's oblivious, and then he jams into me and it hurts. And then I'm thinking this *isn't* right, this *isn't* what I wanted—but it is, you know, him inside of me and all, filling up what's empty. Still, I scooch up on all fours, pull away a little, and then it's like he's getting his balance, getting grounded, because he pushes my shoulders down onto the floor and I'm down there like that, ass high and my shoulders, my chest, my neck and everything are raw, rug burned, and it's like rubbing up against sandpaper, and it hurts, every bit of it, front and back, it all hurts. But I wanted this, right? My nose starts to run, and I fumble around to wipe it with the back of my hand and I'm crying a little, too. Still, I pretend like I'm digging it, wanting it over more than anything, and Sky is back there pounding and pulling on me and when I hear Emily it's sort of muffled at first, and I suppose that maybe I thought she was still down there in her room, doing church-steeple-people or maybe reading her comics, but then it gets louder and then loud enough over all of our body slapping and Sky grunting that I know even before I turn around but can't quite see from there, even before I lift up and look down and through the mess of our bodies, through my legs then his, I know that Emily is there at the door. And she is, of course, eyes wide and mouth moving, but then she's gone, and the front door opens and slams and even though the thunder has stopped, it's pouring out there so what else can I do but go myself. So I pull away from Sky and his face is priceless, skin like milk and blue-green eyes dark as stones and beautiful. He looks surprised.

"Emily," I mumble and roll away and pull into my clothes and he's all the while still there on his knees and naked.

"What the fuck," he says. He's mad now, and not like I blame him, but still. And I can see him eyeballing the safe there in the closet, but I can't be bothered with that. I know what's going to happen, but it's like a force set into motion that can't be stopped. "Go ahead," I want to say, but whatever I say can't possibly make any difference.

I know where to go to find Emily. I run to the park, the big houses a beige wet blur around me, my bare feet smacking the sidewalk, smooshing worms all the way. "Emily," I say, but I don't yell it. The rain is letting up now, and if I'd look, there might even be a patch of blue in the dark. But that's not what I'm looking for.

When I find Emily she's soaked through and tangled up in the big web, legs and hands sticking through the openings, face mashed against the ropes. When she sees me, her eyes get bright and it's like she's already forgotten what just happened.

"Emily," I say. She smiles a little, only her lips are pressed almost shut because of how tangled she is.

"Got stuck," she says through her clenched mouth.

"Yeah," I say. My chest aches, from the running I'd like to think, but I know that's not it.

I pull this way and that and an arm comes loose, then a leg.

"Helping me," Emily says.

I nod, but of course I'm lying. See, even as I start to unwind the crisscross of netting, I know that I can't help her. Not really. And the more I tug, the more she gets free and then she's laughing. And it's a real laugh this time, a big old belly laugh, low and full. So there's Emily in the air, caught up in the web, and here's me on the ground with my toes in the mud and she's laughing and—what do you think?—I'm laughing, too. I'm laughing so hard my eyes are streaming, my whole damn body is shaking. It's funny, don't you think? Goddamn hilarious how Emily, sweet, slow, laughing Emily thinks that *I* can help *her*. But me—small, smart, human person—I know the truth. And the truth is—now it kills me to tell you this—the truth is, I'm absolutely no help at all.

HAND THING

This friend of mine only has one hand. No big deal, really, only I didn't notice at first. We met through friends one night—Girls' Night—in a bar; she gave me a soft left-handed squeeze, not a real shake. We drank together, threw back shots and checked out the back pockets of the guys as they leaned on the bar, as they chose songs off the jukebox. She lifted her left hand constantly, in a fist, in a wave, smiled wide, and sucked the guys in. Magnet, one of my friends—her friend—said. Guy magnet. And why not? Wasn't like she was ugly or anything. Very cute, as a matter of fact. Blond and little. The kind of girl makes girls like me feel big and too dark. Like even though there's less of her, she's got more to offer. But then again, there was that hand thing.

I don't know how I saw it. She was really good at distracting you from it, good at keeping your eyes on the lifted hand, the real hand, the only hand; good at keeping your eyes on her smile. The other hand—or not-hand—she kept behind her right hip mostly. Or in a pocket. She used it to lean back against things, kept it between her and the wall. And when I did see it, see what wasn't there, it was just a glimpse, a quick take that landed on a wrist, then nothing, and I started for a second, a flinch maybe, I don't know, but she never said anything, and me either. But I couldn't help but wonder if she saw me, saw me look, look again, look away. I'm pretty sure she did, something makes me think they always do, these people without a hand or something else so different it always sort of knocks the pins out from under whoever is looking. I bet they get used to it, that little pause, that stop-action before it all starts up again, whatever was going on before. Like nothing's different; like nothing's been exposed. Or maybe some people've got the brass enough to say something: What happened to your hand? Wow, you've only got one hand.

Maybe she could go on like that, with just one hand and no one knowing, it not making any big difference until maybe she needed to do something that pretty much took more than one hand, a hand and a wrist at least. Like putting on a coat. Or carrying a big pot of boiling water.

Later I told my uncle about my friend, told him about the hand and no hand, about not seeing it at first, and not knowing why it made a difference enough now to even bring it up. And he told me about this girl he knew a long time ago, girl he kind of liked, girl he dated once. Same thing with her. She had no hand on one arm. Well, that's not entirely true, she had a sort of hand, a couple of knuckles and a stub of thumb. And he didn't notice at first, either.

They met at a party. They danced, they hugged, they kissed. They were drinking a lot, and it was dark, but still, he thought he would've seen. But he didn't. And he invited her over for a date, not that night, but another one. He made her dinner.

She was really pretty and they were having lots of fun, laughing and eating, and she had some extra fine manners, one hand in the lap; he thought wasn't she polite. But it was the hand that was not all there, he figured out later. Still, it was good manners. And somewhere in the middle of the meal, for some reason—they were laughing and joking and eating and drinking—she just comes out and says, "Well, I only have one hand." And he says "Yeah, right." And she giggles a little and lifts up her napkin with the almost-hand from her lap, dabs at the sides of her mouth and says, "No really," and peels the napkin from her fist, and he sees, for the first time, those lonely little knuckles and a tiny thumb that's so pink, pink as her lips. And he just looks, for seconds, not many, but too many, he figures out later, and doesn't say anything. Probably his mouth is hanging open, too, but he couldn't say for sure. But then he says, "Oh," and asks if she wants more wine or maybe some coffee. And he's rubbing both his own hands into his own napkin, trying not to be stupid. And she lifts up out of her chair and leans all the way across to him over the tiny table and slides her big hand down the side of his face, and presses the warm, smooth skin of her forearm (the arm with the almost-hand) against the back of his neck and draws him to her close, and puts her mouth on his, her tongue pushing past both their lips and tasting sweet, hot, and then draws her head back just a little and breathes some fresh, cinnamon breath into his face and says, "I get along fine with what I do have." And he can't argue, so he pushes back his own chair and moves to her, and lifts her across the one room of his apartment to the couch where they press against each other in all of their clothes, and sweat and let out deep, wet sighs until the sky starts to glow outside, and the birds start making noise, and he says "You better go." And she says, "I don't have to, you know." And he kisses her again, and runs his hand over her blouse, over her jeans, and everything is wet and warm, and he pulls away, against the back of the couch, and says, "Yes, yes you do. You really do." And he smiles so she knows it's not her, it's not her hand. It just is. He's being nice. Not wanting to go too far on their first date. Not wanting to take advantage.

He walks her to her car and holds the door open for her, watches her slide her ass, the one he'd just had his hands all over, over the seat. She reaches her right hand across her body and rolls down the window to kiss him one more time. He watches as she takes hold of the steering wheel with the almost-hand and turns the key with the other. She smiles up at him, and he can't help but love that she is so pretty, that she smells so good, and her smell is still on him. And he watches how she sort of grips the wheel with the tiny thumb and shifts out of park, and he says, "I'll call you."

But he never does.

My uncle was forty when he told me that story, and it all happened when he was just a little more than twenty. He told me he still thought about the girl, knew that he blew it by not calling her, never knew anyone before or since who would hold him so tight with an arm at his low back, pressing and pressing, a soft hand at the back of his neck, fingers at the edges of his hair. But what did all that matter now? What could he change?

And I wondered what I had that might make a man remember me twenty years after our first—our only—date. And then I figured maybe it's what you don't have that makes them remember.

And my friend at the bar with all those guys coming up to her, on to her, what did they think about later when she released them, sent them on their way and they left the place without ever knowing, without ever seeing? Did they go home and think of her, picture her in their minds with two hands? One cupping their balls, the other brushing against the hairs on their chests? And what about those who did know, who did see? What did they conjure up later when they went home alone, climbed between the sheets with no one else there? Maybe they made it a different picture. More real, you know, with her there next to them, slipping the smooth stub of her wrist into the narrow slot between belly and fly, using the good hand, the only hand, somewhere else. Or maybe they tied her up, took both those wrists and crossed them over one another and strapped them up with something—although I'm not entirely sure how that would work, tying someone up without the width of the palm to hold the binding in place—then pulled her long and sort of arched her back against the mattress, got the hands out of the picture like that. Out of the way.

Or maybe, in their minds, she still had both hands. They saw her the way they wanted her to be, which was what they believed to be whole, because it was a fantasy, after all. Their fantasy.

And did anyone ever make it through that first night, that first meeting without catching on, without catching sight, and get past all the others who were drawn to her, get the phone number, get the date, without ever getting the real picture first? Like my uncle. What happened when they did notice? Did they say something? Did she?

Sometimes, I guess, the guy would already like her before he noticed, already think she was worth getting to know better. And maybe he'd see that little empty space where the hand should be somehow, see her swing that arm out when she got bumped into, see her push it quickly back into her pocket. Maybe that's when he'd turn to see what else was there, what other choices he had. Like me next to her. Big and dark, but whole, it looked like from where he stood. He'd do a quick check, I'd hold my beer with both hands tight around the bottle, hoping he'd see something else. But even with all my parts showing, something might still be missing. So he'd go on and ask for her phone number. And he'd call her.

Or maybe he wouldn't call her.

Because, after all, there was that hand thing.

THE WAY IT REALLY WENT

One thing about cancer—and anyone who knows anyone who's had it knows this, too—it's the name of it that gets you sick. Here's what I mean:

A guy goes through his everyday life, not feeling bad or anything, not feeling anything different at all except one day feeling a little hard bubble of something under his skin. Say he's in the shower, soaping up all the parts he usually does, thinking about how he hates to have to ever get out from under the warm stream of water, hates to have to get a move on and put his uniform on and go sit on the little stool he sits on all day, doing the exact same job he's been doing for fifteen years, selling the same tickets to the same people for the same buses going to the same places. On automatic pilot, more or less, trying not to let it bother him, the monotony, the sameness, but knowing that it does. And then, all of a sudden, something is different, something has changed. And what it is is this little raising of flesh here under his arm on his side. A pebble, it feels like. Tough under the fingers, but it doesn't hurt. *Huh*, he says to himself and fingers it under the soapy slide of skin before he rinses off and shrugs it off and dries off and goes about his day. Only every once in a while, his fingers find their way back to that spot under his arm, play over the spot, pushing and wondering if the thing's bigger or smaller than it was the last time he messed with it an hour or so ago. When he gets home he pulls the tails of his shirt out of his pants and steps up close to the full-length mirror on the back of the bedroom door, studies the spot but doesn't see anything, not even the bump of it unless he uses two fingers of one hand on either side of it to stretch the skin back over the area—and then what he sees he can't tell if it's real or imagined it's such a small deviation from the flat, pale plane of his side. *A cyst, maybe,* he thinks, and tries to ignore it, doesn't tell anyone, not even his wife because she'd think he was whining and that makes her mad, and besides it's probably nothing. And the next day and the next when he takes a shower he presses on it, squeezes it, and gets to doing that so regularly that it becomes part of the routine, as mindless as the act of rinsing the shampoo out of his thick black hair. He still doesn't feel bad, not any more tired or achy than usual, just the pains of getting near forty and not doing enough besides sitting and watching TV and life from his couch at home, his stool at work.

But then one day it hurts. Really hurts. Like a stab of something when he presses on it, a sharpness that radiates up and down from his armpit to the lowest edge of his ribs. He remembers what it was like when he had that plantar wart once and it got so painful that he could hardly step on the ball of his right foot. And even though it hurts, this thing, maybe a wart, he still doesn't feel too bad, although he has been getting sort of tired lately. But he imagines that's because he doesn't sleep too well anymore. Dreams of dogs biting him and sinking their teeth in under his arm—shining slivers of enamel left in his skin when he finally pulls the beasts away—shake him up enough that he forces himself awake and keeps his eyes wide open and fixed on the ceiling until he's sure he won't fall back in with the dogs again.

So when it gets to hurting, the man makes an appointment with the doctor. And when the doctor asks, he realizes that he can't remember when he first noticed it, can't remember when it wasn't there, part of him. And after this test and that, the doctor tells him what he already knows, says the word in a stream of other possible words. And the man knows it's this one, recognizes the word that had been in his mind all the while, even though he'd never actually said it, even to himself. And the man's surprised that he isn't surprised by what the doctor tells him. Yet, familiar as the word is when he hears it, it still shakes him up, and he sits for a long while on the cold examining table, left alone in the room to dress. Only he can't move. Not voluntarily. He listens to his mind telling his legs to stand now, his hands to reach for his clothes; he even prods himself *Come on, get going* out loud, but it's like he's stuck there, trapped in the sterile white room by the word, trapped in this body which he thought he knew and trusted. Trapped in the body that had turned on him, and now turned on him again by not standing, not taking him out of there, but instead doing its own thing, shaking uncontrollably from toe to head, shivering and shuddering so hard that the paper of the examining robe rattles in the quiet.

And then, for the first time since he found that little bubble under his skin, for the first time ever, perhaps, he says the word himself. *Cancer*, he says, whispering the name as he shakes in the paper robe in the quiet, white room. And then, when the man names it, that's when he gets sick.

When Jim called before he left work at the station and said we needed to talk, I knew he didn't mean we'd have a real conversation where he says something, then I do—but more than likely he wanted me to stay quiet while he talked. I knew something was up, I saw the signs. He'd drift away somewhere while we sat in front of the late news, his fingers strumming his ribs, his eyes blanking out. He wouldn't answer me when I'd say something then, not hearing. Ignoring, maybe. It doesn't matter which. The thing is, it was me who always did the talking anyway. But now I figured he probably wanted me to sit tight and listen while he said one of those three-word sentences most women live in dread of hearing: *This isn't working* or *I've met someone*. Like I said, there were signs.

The way I imagined it would go:

At Anchors Inn, the only rib joint in town and Jim's favorite restaurant (never mind that I'd given up red meat), he would be on his side of the table looking twitchy, the sweat shining in his thick black curls; I'd be on mine, dressed up for once, figure what the hell, might as well step out of those old jeans and T-shirt I live in mostly and slip into the black mini-skirt pushed to the back of the closet. Heels, too. Figure if it's going to be him leaving me, he better damn sure know what he's leaving behind.

I'd sit on my red vinyl bench across the red plaid table-cloth from my ten-year husband and listen to him hemming and hawing around those words—*This, er, I've, uh....* I imagined when he finally did say it—his brown eyes focused on a spot some-where off to the side of my head, his Adam's apple bobbing—I'd just smile big and nod nicely, and stand up and lean over to kiss the top of his head. Good luck, I'd say, and leave him there, walk away and leave him getting an eyeful of my good side.

The way it really went:

I sat in the flickering light of the fake lanterns tacked up on the rough-paneled walls and watched Jim squirm. He looked small in his white shirt and black tie, his bus ticket sell-er's uniform, and damn if it didn't look like he might cry. He kept blinking and clearing his throat, and I waited for him to say something, like it seemed I was always waiting for him. I used to finish his sentences for him; it was as if he just didn't

have enough words in him to make it through a whole conversation sometimes. But I got tired of that, like I got tired of the
other things: the way he pretended not to stare at every other
woman in the neighborhood—from the high school girls working
at the Stop 'n' Shop with their tight bodies and too-tight jeans
to the new moms pushing their buggies'-full, their ripe boobs
bouncing; the nights I went to bed hours ahead of him so he
could watch the round-up shows after the games, and then the
highlights on the late news, and then whatever sports they'd be
playing in some other part of the world in the middle of the night
that he could get on that damned cable; the pools of water on
the bathroom floor that I'd slip in every morning when I went
in after him to pick up his towels, put the seat down, wipe the
toothpaste splatters off the mirror. Like a Goddamn bad rerun
our life was, and I couldn't even remember anymore when things
weren't exactly the same.

But that night at the Inn, things seemed different somehow.
And as I sat there waiting for Jim to talk, my heart pounded in
me. A good pound. A life's-about-to-change-get-ready-it's-your-
turn kind of pound. It nearly made me giddy. And, God help me,
I felt like laughing. But of course I didn't.

"I..." Jim started finally, after our busboy came by to fill our
water glasses and put our place settings down.

"-'m leaving," I finished the sentence in my head for him.
But I kept my lips pressed tight together. And Jim, after that first
false start, closed his own mouth and pushed back into his seat,
then opened his mouth long enough to gulp down some water,
then closed it again, his eyes skittering around, touching everything but mine.

Maybe I should have left him. Not like the thought hadn't
crossed my mind a million times over the last, oh, not ten years
(because the first two were actually pretty good I think, I don't
remember how or why, only I have this feeling that there was
something more than just pleasant about them) but in the last

eight years I'd often considered going. Still, there's a certain comfort in what's familiar, and Jim was definitely familiar. We'd known each other since the sixth grade. He was the first boy I let slide his hand into my shirt, under the bra, back in freshman year behind the rear door of the field house. I looked across the table at Jim's hands. At the half-moons under his nails, the ones that meant money or luck, I'd heard somewhere. At the long, sleek white digits fidgeting with the spoon, the knife. His hands were what made me fall for him for real in the first place. Even before that day when he slipped one inside the cool cotton of my bra and it felt so wonderfully warm and smooth, a press of palm so real and alive, like nothing I'd ever felt before. When he slid that palm over my nipple we both took in air at precisely the same moment, a gasp so quick and deep that he just about snatched his hand back, and would have if I hadn't hugged it to me, pushed my whole self up against it and him, wanting the feeling of his electric warmth to take me over entirely until we had to pull apart and run around to the front entrance and get to homeroom before the second bell rang.

His hands were clean, always, the fingers long and solid. They looked good holding things. In seventh grade he came over to our house with a big brown casserole of beans and ham from his mom, an offering of sympathy the morning after my dad died, and when I went to the door and found him there, shifting from foot to foot, his nose red and runny, maybe from the cold October mistiness, I couldn't look in his eyes when he said he was sorry, *You know, about your dad and all, I mean*, so instead I focused in on his hands, white and strong around the heavy brown dish; and they looked so perfect, the nail beds pink and long and healthy, my heart broke and filled in the same instant, and I couldn't help but break and sob, and he dropped that big old casserole, beans and slimy ham all over our front stoop, and he put his hands on me, on my back, in my hair, on my face, and how could I help but love him then?

But all that was years before. Years before we went together, broke up, got back together, had a child, lost a child, and so on. It all somehow seemed like an inalterable progression. After Jim and I were married, we seemed to just keep going on with our lives, nothing changing, unless you count that day of the accident and how after that we clung to each other at first, tried to start over, to have another baby with not a bit of luck, then stopped talking nearly except when I nagged him, hissed at him, and then stopped sleeping together entirely, sharing a bed, but not bodies, and how I started stepping out, finding someone or other to hold me, someone or other to want me. So even though I didn't ever go anywhere, I guess I had been doing my own leaving for a while, and now I figured Jim could leave me and we could get on with things.

I watched our waitress at the next table pull a long pepper mill out of her red apron pocket in an elegant arc, and twist the big thing over the plate of a woman with hair so black it was blue. The woman lifted her hand in a small wave. "When," she said.

Jim picked up his menu, put the plastic wall of it up between us. "What're you gonna have?" he said. The first full sentence since we'd been there.

"I'm not too hungry," I said, not even bothering to open my menu. "I'll just go for the salad bar."

"Yeah," Jim said and put the menu down again. His lips pulled down at the corners and a line creased deeply across his forehead. "Maybe I will, too. Red meat's not too good for you."

Now here was something different. Jim was the kind of man who joked about not getting enough fat, not having a high enough cholesterol level. "More salt," he'd say at the movies when he ordered popcorn, "keep pouring, keep pouring! I can still see some yellow from the butter."

And it was at this moment that I got scared.

"Jim—?"

"I went to the doctor today," he said and turned his head toward the bar, away from me. He began to roll up his sleeve. There was a purple patch of skin spreading out from under a bandaid in the crook of his elbow. The back of my neck got cold.

And then he said it. Three words, the number I knew there would be. But not the right three words.

"They found something."

An odd sensation seeped through me. I don't know what you'd call it, but I know I'd felt it twice before. That time when my mom came home and told me what happened on the afternoon my dad died on the job, a heart attack that took him down to the cement floor of the bays of the trucking company right before lunch time, made him dead before the first of the guys on the way back from the cafeteria found him down there, cold and totally empty of breath. That time, and the day of our daughter's accident.

My eyes burned, and I swallowed and swallowed, trying to get that thing out of my throat so that I could talk.

"It's just a lump," Jim said finally, reaching one of those perfect hands across the table to me. His fingertips touched the white knuckles of my own hand gripping the edge of the table. His voice was soft now. It sounded young and concerned. Scared, maybe.

"What the hell does that mean, Jim?" And here's the thing, I heard my own voice get too loud, raggedy. And the feeling that covered me a minute before was burning off into anger. Even I knew this wasn't right, this wasn't what Jim needed from me right then, to be pissed off at him. Pissed off *again*, for chrissakes. But I was. And maybe I was at least a little mad at myself then for not seeing this coming, for imagining something else, protecting myself from the wrong thing by imagining something entirely impossible, Jim having an affair—boring, settled Jim, as loyal and unambitious as a fat old house dog. Mostly, though, I was mad at him. "What's 'it's just a lump' supposed to fucking mean?"

Our waitress—Christy, her brass name pin said—was at our tableside then, her hand on her pepper mill, just doing her job but caught in our little moment and frozen there, it looked like. It was all I could do not to reach over and snatch the damn wooden pepper club from her and swing it around in an elegant arc over Jim's head. I'll give him a lump.

"Uh, I guess you need more time," Christy said when I turned my face to her. The fire I felt in my forehead must have shone in my eyes. She patted the table twice and smiled her good waitress smile and backed away.

I looked back at Jim, at his skinny neck in the wide starched white collar. His fingers had slipped from my knuckles but his hand stayed stretched across the wide table, the pink pillows of his palm up. He blinked and blinked, his deep brown eyes fogging and clearing; his lips worked like he was trying to say something but couldn't. The spot under the Band-Aid on his outstretched arm looked colored on, a fake bruise.

"Ah, shit," I said, when the strangle hold of it all finally let go of my throat. I took his hand in my own, startled by how strange and how familiar the skin-to-skin warmth and smoothness of it felt. Jim tilted his head up and watched me stand. He looked so damn small there surrounded by red vinyl, a boy at the end of the marred arm. "Come on," I said and jiggled our hands held together like a double-sized fist. "Let's go home."

Back at the house, we let go of one another's hands just long enough to undress and—Jim in his T-shirt and boxers, me in my panties—we got into bed on our backs and on our own sides. Our hands found their way to one another across the span of cold sheet. Jim fell fast and hard into sleep. I lay still and silent, stared at the black flatness of the ceiling and wondered if something as routine as sleep would ever come to me again. And when it did, I didn't notice until I was pulled out of it, away from dreams with no movement, still pictures of people and objects vaguely familiar yet unrecognizable. Jim's crying woke me, but not him. He whimpered and shuddered, but didn't come to, so I slid over the mattress and into him, pressed myself against the back I'd gotten used to having turned to me at night. Each sob shook me, and I held on, clucked in a way that came natural to me, even though our bodies, pressed together, felt changed—my own softer and fleshier than whenever the last time we touched like this was, his thinner and somehow brittle. His shirt was soaked through, so I pulled it up his back and over his head, and in his sleep he let me. The slick skin of him was hot and cold at the same time, but I stayed close until he felt just-right warm against me. The crying stopped and gave way to even breathing, heavy and thick with sleep, and when he's five minutes' calm, I run my hand up his side, smoothing the skin until I feel it. And it's true, there's not much there, a couple stitches over a pea of sickness, and I wish that I could bite it, take it between my teeth and pull back quick and hard until it's out of him and in my mouth and then I could spit it out. Into the toilet, I think, and I'd flush it away and when Jim woke up it would be gone, and he'd be old Jim again, same old same old, and I'd be Annie, just like before—whatever, whoever, that was.

The surgery came four days later. In the recovery room everyone was smiling, Jim even, ready to believe that was that. "Optimistic" was the word the doctors used then. I wanted to believe, too, but the tightness I'd felt at the Inn had turned into a knot, a hard blister of dread. And then the day after the surgery when they read his tests, the blood work and lymph nodes, they found more.

They say what doesn't kill you will only make you stronger, but I'm not sure that goes for chemotherapy. Jim couldn't eat from queasiness, and after his daily shots he'd vomit up all that nothing. From my cold plastic chair outside the examining room, it was like I could hear his bones rattle with the dry heaves. When he'd come back through the doorway, gray and wobbly, I'd go to him and curl under his arm, make myself a crutch for the slow move down the long bright hallway to the exit. It was like we used to walk, back in high school, wrapped into one another so tightly that if one tipped, both would.

At home one day I heard the shower running, but it sounded like it was falling straight down, like no one was moving under it. I put my ear against the door and listened hard. "Jim?" I whispered against the wood. And then I heard that sound of his crying, a soft whimpering, and the quiet distress of it ran through me like ice water. "Jim?" I said again, a little louder this time, and rattled the doorknob. He sniffed. "Yes," he said, I heard the shoring up under the word, the effort it took to keep it steady. I stepped inside the bathroom, waved my hand in front of my face to clear a path in the steam. "Honey?" I pulled back the shower curtain and found him sitting there on the floor of the tub, knees pulled up to his chest, arms wrapped tightly around them. "Go away," he said into the space between his knees, and from where I was I could see the white of his scalp through his hair, something I'd never seen before. I stood there, my hand still holding back the curtain, not sure what to do next.

"I said go away." He didn't raise his voice, there was no edge in it. He said it like a plain and simple fact. But I couldn't go.

"Jim," I said again, almost a whisper, running out of words myself this time, and put a hand on the back of his neck. He tilted his face up to me. His eyes were rimmed and red, his cheeks slick with steam and tears and snot.

"I can't even take a fucking shower anymore," he said softly, and his eyes began to fill. "I'm just so damn tired," he put his head back on his knees and his shoulders shook. So I climbed in there with him, right down on the porcelain next to him, jeans, T-shirt, socks and all, pulled him into a circle I made with my legs, into the circle of my arms. We rocked there for a good long while, him crying and me thinking about crying but unable to, I hadn't shed a tear since the news first came. I wasn't trying to be strong or anything—I knew that in some long-guarded, hard-sided spot near the blister-knot inside me, I wanted to sob. But I couldn't. And then we lay out long in the tub, felt the water pour down over us, clutched together chest-to-chest, legs tucked up and around one another so we could fit in the small space. When the water ran cold, I reached up and turned it off, but we lay there still, who knows how long; and later, much later, we stood up together and I pulled off my own clothes and turned the water back on and held him with one arm and ran the soap over him with my free hand. Even in its whiteness and stick-thinness, his body felt familiar under my hands, and when I bent to my knees and soaped his balls, his dick, the long, hard muscles of his thighs, I couldn't help but remember the times when we'd done this for fun, lathered each other up and slipped our bodies against one another. And his dick remembered too, because it stiffened some, but not much, and I kissed its little head for old time's sake before I stood up again and hugged Jim to me while I reached around him to scrub his back.

He sagged against me while I washed him, his arms resting over my shoulders and his legs shaking under his weight. But then I felt a gathering of the energy in his body, and he pulled back from me just far enough to look into my face.

"I'm really sorry, Annie," he said, his voice low and thick.

There were a lot of things I'd wanted him to be sorry for over the years. Sorry for not being able to keep a better hold on our daughter. Sorry for giving up on our having another kid without ever talking to me about it. Sorry for my feeling like I had to go out on him, look elsewhere for what I thought he should be giving me. Sorry for standing by while all we had that had been warm and familiar turned to cold, cold routine. Sorry for us. Sorry for me. But this? This was not his fault. There was nothing here for him to be sorry over.

The water poured down on us, cold again, and I moved in for some of Jim's warmth. And when I did, I felt myself slip. Jim lifted a hand to me and I grabbed it, held onto it, and then slid it over my breast. I wished he could push his fingers under my skin and through the bones that cross over my heart and find that knot inside me. I wanted him to rub away its hardness. He cupped his other hand behind my neck, and we pressed together. "I'm sorry," he said again. I wanted to tell him it's okay. *Don't worry, it's okay.* But standing with his hands—those same old perfect hands—on me, holding me, keeping me steady, I couldn't say anything. So I nodded. That's all I was able to do. Just nod. I couldn't do anything more.

THE TWIN

Ernie heard the yelling first as he climbed out of the front seat of the old Toyota. "Buy American," some punk or other was always yelling at them, him and Bert when they drove past the park or the high school. But that wasn't what he heard when he arrived at seven that morning to open up the ice cream parlor. From the parking lot, the yelling sounded like wailing. Or howling. A desperate, long, low-pitched sob.

Ernie thought maybe it came from the storefront meditation church, the Temple of Air. The ice cream parlor and temple shared a wall in the small strip shopping center. There was always singing or praying or some sort of joyful noise going on over there, sometimes yelling even, especially on a Saturday, their main day of worship. But this was a little too early for the temple, and the parking lot was empty. The white stripes between the spaces looked like they needed painting, which they did; they were much too ghostly and weak on the faded blacktop to keep the cars apart. On a busy temple morning, which this was sure to be when the sun moved up into a warm spot that would burn off the early mist, cars would be parked in nothing near order, spilling over the lines and squeezed in too tightly, or parked at odd angles meant to protect side panels and doors from bumps and dings. It about drove Ernie crazy.

But the yelling. The sobbing. Ernie stood beside the Toyota for a minute to try to hear where it was coming from. It sounded like it was in front of him in the shopping center somewhere, but also above him somehow. And then it stopped.

"Hmmph," he exhaled, and turned the key in the lock of the car door (a habit left over from the city) and then spun the big jangling ring of keys around until he found the one for the ice cream shop. He stepped up to the door and put the key in the lock, turned it, then pushed the door open so that the bell over it rang out prettily.

"Hey! Fuck! Hey!"

The yelling rose over the hum of the freezers and stopped Ernie still under the bell. "What the...?" he mumbled.

"Hey, help! Back here! Help!"

It wasn't Ernie's morning to open the shop; it was Bert's. Those weren't their real names, Bert and Ernie, but the ones they'd taken on when they took off from the city, from the Chicago Mercantile Exchange where they shared the position of back office manager at Bronstein Financials for six years before they got the idea to slide a couple of winning trades into an account with their real names, Robert and Henry Saltzman, on it. Well, it started with a couple of trades—but then when no one noticed, and it seemed so effortless, so easy, unlike the rest of their days filled with brokers and clients bothering them all the time, all the time, calling on the phone and standing over their desks clearing their throats, tapping their feet, yelling and bossing and whining—they did it again. And again. A winner here, a winner there, and suddenly they had something, some money, a tidy little sum, a significant retirement package, as they liked to call it. And still no one noticed. Why would they?

Robert and Henry handled the statements, checked for errors and out-trades and margin calls, and this would be the sort of thing they would watch for in everyone else's accounts. But then the Commodity Futures Trading Commission showed up for a routine audit, and Robert and Henry left the job at lunchtime, which was unusual since they mostly ate lunch in the break room, sharing sandwiches out of one bag, chips and sodas out of another. It was hard to tell them apart sometimes, they were identical twins who, even near thirty, wore identical glasses and dressed in look-alike suits and similar ties made from the same polyester fabrics. So that day when the CFTC came in, Robert excused himself at lunch to go to the dentist, he said, and for fifteen minutes Henry (dumb with nerves) sat in the break room with two sandwiches and two RC Colas and a baggie filled with greasy potato chips and then, as Robert had instructed him to, got up and went into the men's room in the hall, and then out to the elevators and down to the lobby, and some of the brokers said later that they thought they'd seen him get in a cab, but maybe it was Robert, it was hard to tell. And then they packed their bags, four identical Samsonites with silver metal locks, and loaded them into the trunk of the Toyota and pulled out of the under-ground garage of the apartment building with the parquet floors and low ceilings and wide windows where they'd lived together since their sophomore year in college at Circle Campus where they'd enrolled to stay out of the draft, and drove and drove until they got tired—which wasn't too far because neither of them liked to drive very much.

And they ended up here.

So today it was Bert's turn to open up the ice cream parlor; they took turns on Saturdays coming in early. But Bert's allergies were acting up since things were starting to bloom, and this was one thing the men didn't share, allergies, so Ernie had offered to go in.

"Come on, man! Fuck!"

Ernie had never been partial to swearing. That had been a real liability working in the financial markets; the traders were all so rude.

"W-where are you?" Ernie called out into the dark. He still couldn't quite place the sound, but it might have been coming from the storage room. Or maybe the roof. He was aware then, like he always was, of the smell of the place. It surprised and delighted him, even now, after these years, the sweet scent of this place where he worked. Sugar and milk, the cookie smell of ice cream cones. So different from the Mercantile Exchange where things always smelled like men's sweat and socks and stale cigarette smoke, burnt coffee. Today though, in the shop there was another odor that cut through the soft sugary scent; it smelled like copper a little, like wet pennies. Ernie sniffed and called again: "Where are you?"

"Here, man, here! In back." The last words sounded quieter than the others, deflated.

Ernie lightly stepped over the black and white tiles until he was behind the counter. He reached over the cash register to the light switches, and threw them all up. The place filled with the glare of fluorescence on shining steel and bright white walls.

"Fuck, man, shit! My eyes!"

And then there was no doubt. The voice was definitely coming from the storage and prep room, in the rear of the shop, near the big freezers. Ernie tiptoed back.

The room appeared empty except for all the stuff, the paper cups and boxes of spoons, plastic boats, sugar cones and safety cones. The metal racks of paper napkins and fresh dish-cloths from the linen service; toilet paper and the toweling they put in those holders near the slop sink and in the bathrooms, big round rolls of it with a blue stripe down the center. Ernie saw nothing there among the things that kept the parlor running efficiently and neatly, no one that could have said the bad words that he was certain he had heard.

"Man, finally. Shit, finally."

Ernie looked up. A head poked out from the ceiling like a *piñata*. From the air duct, actually. A man's head, or a boy's maybe, with too much hair. It hung down from the top of the boy's upside down head, and Ernie's first thought was that he should be wearing a hairnet, the boy; it was unsanitary all of that greasy hair hanging down over the paper cups and plastic spoons and sugar cones. He followed the line of it down and then saw on the floor beneath the hair a metal grating that was usually stuck in the ceiling where the air came through, and it looked as though it had been ripped from its place among the ceiling tiles, bits of the foam-like material still clinging to its edges. And on closer inspection, Ernie noticed the white dust everywhere. And the dark spots of something wet.

"Oh dear," he said, like he did when he got nervous or mad or sad or excited. "Oh dear."

"Fuckin'A" the boy said. His mouth was where his eyebrows should have been, since he was upside down, and it looked to Ernie like his forehead was talking.

"Language, please," Ernie said.

"What?" The boy's forehead said.

"Language. Please. Watch your language."

And the boy shifted some above Ernie, tilted his head at an odd angle like he was trying to turn it over, trying to right himself, or maybe just his head, so that he could see Ernie better, right-side up at least.

"Ow, fuck," the boy said, and then, "Sorry. Man, sorry. Hey, help, can you?"

Ernie moved closer to the boy, and when he did, he recognized him. He wasn't a boy, really, but a young man who was just past his teens when Ernie first saw him a few years before at the edge of the parking lot where those kids hang out late at night. His name was Eric or something. Jared. Ernie shook his head. That wasn't it. Derek! Yes, Derek. And his last name started with a "J", Ernie was pretty certain. One of those Bohemian names they all had around town.

"What are you doing?" Ernie asked. It hurt to strain his neck back like he had to in order to talk with the man, so he dragged over a step stool, the one he used to get to the extra boxes of napkins he stored on the high shelves. He climbed until he was nearly face-to-face with the fellow. Forehead to chin at least. The man's eyes were bloodshot and his face was very white. He was perspiring.

"I'm stuck," he said. His voice was quiet now that Ernie was so close. He, Derek, sounded spent. The wet penny smell wafted from him.

"Yes, I see," Ernie said, and he peered into the air duct above Derek and saw that one shoulder was wedged against the ceiling and an arm was bent funny with something, blood, Ernie could see now, tracing small lines down the fingers that looked like they were sticking out of the man's neck somehow. "Very stuck, it looks like." He reached up to touch Derek's fingers and the man's eyes went wide as a frightened cat's. "Don't worry," Ernie said, even though he couldn't think of any reason at all why Derek wouldn't worry; this was a bad situation, a real jam, that's for sure. The tips of the fellow's fingers were clammy and cold. "Hmm," Ernie said, and pulled his hand back. And he couldn't help it, he smelled his own fingers, discreetly, and there was that sharp coppery smell. "Well," he said, and he backed down the rungs of the step stool. "We'll have to do something, won't we?"

And Derek made a movement with his head that looked like a nod, only upside down and very, very small. He closed his eyes.

"Are you tired?" Ernie asked. It seemed like the right question, a polite inquiry.

"Yes," the man said. His breath smelled of beer and sick.

"Yes, of course," Ernie said. He couldn't help but think of himself as a host to this man stuck in his air duct. And even though he and his brother served ice cream to dozens of people every day, the way Ernie felt in relation to this fellow was not exactly the same thing. On hot, busy days, the ice cream parlor had a continuous stream of patrons, and the twins worked like a short, efficient assembly line: Ernie scooping and Bert taking the money and making change, and then Bert scooping and Ernie at the cash register. On those days there wasn't time for much small talk and pleasantries. On slower days, there was always something to do when they weren't dipping cones. "Got time to lean, got time to clean," Bert would say while he flipped through a fishing magazine at a table and Ernie busied himself with a towel, a mop, the push broom. Now, though, before the door was open and the customers lined up, before Bert came in and things shifted under the weight of their shared responsibilities, Ernie found himself considering Derek a guest—not a patron, but a visitor. And since Ernie and his brother Bert never had visitors (they were, after all, on the run) this feeling of playing host was not entirely familiar to Ernie. Surprisingly pleasant, though. Because if Ernie were to think about it at all, he would have to admit that this life he and his brother had designed for themselves, this life of work and not much else, of hiding from their past and keeping their present small, close, easy to share and to manage—Ernie would have to admit to himself (but never to Bert) that he was, in fact, lonely.

When Henry and Robert first arrived in New Hope those years ago, they stayed at the High Hope Motor Court located on the wooded slope of one of the hills at the edge of town. They'd paid for two weeks in advance, in cash, and Robert had signed them in under their real names, but scribbled their signatures so they were essentially illegible—a messiness he prided himself on because he thought it made his name look more important. At the trading firm he'd signed hundreds of checks and thousands of statements, sweeping the pen over the documents with a flourish and a sigh, fully aware that hundreds of thousands of dollars were accounted for or released under indecipherable squiggles and lines made by his own hand.

"What's that say?" The old lady at the desk lifted up her bifocals and leaned closer to the register. Henry could see her scalp where her dyed black hair parted, and the whispery lines of gray on either side of the pink line of flesh. Would they have to dye their own hair, Henry wondered. Clearly they had to become someone other than who they were now. New names, new jobs. New hair? New clothes? Maybe he'd go blond if Robert chose black; he'd take to wearing blue jeans and gym shoes.

The incredible possibility of becoming another person— not just Henry of Robert and Henry, not just one of "the twins" like everyone called them at work, at school, at their apartment in the city, like their parents had called them up until the day Mr. and Mrs. Saltzman loaded their moving van and left the cold winter suburbs for the sunshine of Florida and had skidded off the road in a freak ice storm in Tennessee, leaving behind a tangle of overdrafts and unpaid bills and two grown-up sons to take care of it all—the opportunity to start again as someone other than whom he had been all of his life was exhilarating to Henry. And terrifying. In equal doses. The enormity of it left him without words standing in the tiny office cabin at High Hope Motor Court, fascinated now by the wiry black hairs at the edges of the old woman's upper lip. She looked from one twin to the other and back, blinking as though clearing sleep from her eyes.

"Hubert," Robert said. "Call me Bert."

And Henry was amazed (even after all these years) at how quickly Robert had figured things out, developed a strategy, responded to a problem with a solution. Robert smiled broadly at the woman, all orthodontist-straightened teeth and pink lips and soft eyes. He was the handsome one.

She smiled back, the hairs twitching at the corners of her mouth.

"And this one?" She pointed to the other name. "I can't make it out at all."

"Ernie," Robert said. "Like those puppets on television, only we were Bert and Ernie first. Seagram. Like the whiskey."

Henry tried the new name out in his head, *Ernie, Ernie, Ernie,* and *Seagram, Seagram, Seagram,* and it was okay, close enough.

"That Jewish?" The old lady asked. Her eyes swept over Robert's close-cut auburn curls and landed on Henry's nose, which had a bump made by Robert's elbow, an accident during a foot race when they were kids.

"English," Robert said, still smiling, always smiling, but Henry saw the tightening of muscle in his temple. "Our grandfather was Jewish," Robert said, the story growing so easily that Henry thought for a moment that there might be some truth to it. "We're not religious, though." And they weren't really, although they'd celebrated their bar mitzvah together, like they did everything together, with family and a guest list of nearly one hundred people.

The woman made a noise in her throat, a grunt it sounded like, but then she handed Robert two key rings made from wooden triangles glued together to look like pine trees. And in another few minutes the twins were in their own mold-smelling cabin, one of a half-dozen of them painted Indian red and scattered over the hillside. Wasps buzzed outside the screen door, hovering around a nest in the corner of the awning that was the color of a Dreamsicle. Robert, then Henry, showered, and they unpacked and sat down at the small Formica table near the window (blinds drawn, warm Frescas and bags of crispy cheese puffs in front of them) and began to make a plan.

The fellow, Derek, moaned in a small, quiet way.

"Are you hungry?" Ernie asked.

Derek bobbed his head again. His hair slightly swung beneath him.

"Help me, please."

"Of course," Ernie said. "You must be starving." He spoke with an expanding sense of hospitality, as though the man had just arrived in the shop after a long and complicated journey. Ernie spun around in the back room, turning this way and that trying to solve the problem of his guest's hunger when he decided on the easiest solution. He skipped back out to the front of the shop and saw out the wide windows that a half dozen cars were now in the parking lot. A skinny woman dressed in sky blue climbed out of the driver's side of her Fairmont and waved to Ernie before she crossed the sidewalk to the door of the Temple of Air. Ernie waved back in order to not seem rude, and locked the front door.

He slid open the glass window of the ice cream cooler and looked over the selection of twenty-some flavors in big, round, cardboard tubs. The frozen air lifted from the cooler and fogged his glasses; Ernie removed them and decided on something simple. Orange sherbet. He dug out two scoops from the tub, rolling each into a perfect ball before plopping them into a cardboard cup. He grabbed a pink plastic spoon and went back into the storage room and climbed the step stool to Derek.

"Why are you here?" Ernie asked Derek. He dragged the spoon across a ball of sherbet before lifting it to the man's mouth. It was disconcerting, the way Derek's eyes followed his hand upward, and how his head dropped when he opened his mouth, how his tongue lapped at the spoon from above. Ernie fed him some more, two big spoonfuls, one after the other.

"Whoa," Derek said around a mouthful of orange. "Brain freeze." But the color in his face was pinker than it had been before. He sucked the ice cream and swallowed, his jaw working. "I was gonna rob you. The store, I mean."

Ernie was amazed at the confession, and the ease with which Derek gave it.

"What?"

"Hey, you must've figured by now. And no use pretending." Derek opened his mouth and made a small gesture with his head and the fingers at his neck. "More, please," he said. Ernie filled the spoon again. "I mean, I'm stuck, right? What could I possibly say to the cops besides the truth, right? I've been thinking about it for hours now—"

"Hours?" Ernie said, incredulous. The fellow had been here, upside down and alone and bleeding over the black and white tiled floor of the back room of the ice cream parlor for hours? Hours?

"Yeah. Pretty much since you guys closed up last night. What was that, eleven or so?"

"Eleven-thirty." They were supposed to close at eleven, but a rush came in just before Ernie had a chance to twist the lock on the door, a swarm of folks from the drive-in movie theater close by.

"Plenty of time to try to think up some excuse, but, what excuse could there be, man. You know?" Derek had regained some of his strength from the orange sherbet; his words filled in the space of the storage room. Ernie remembered this about him. Derek was always the loudest in the bunch when he and his friends came in and sat at the small ice cream parlor tables. He was big, too, and he would make the dainty bentwood backed chairs wheeze slightly under his heft, muscle, mostly. And he would sit with his long legs spread out in front of himself, taking up enough room for two or three people. And talk and talk. "So when the cops get here, I'll just tell the truth and suffer the consequences. How bad could it be? That's what I've been thinking all along. I mean, I didn't take anything, yet, right? How bad could it be?" Ernie tried to think of an answer, a response at least, but he was unaccustomed to so much conversation. He and Bert always communicated in that way of twins, never saying much but knowing everything, and as they grew older here in this tiny town, they spoke even less. "I'll just tell the cops everything," Derek said, and shifted in the ceiling and wiggled his fingers. Bits of dust fell into the cup of sherbet, and a small drop of blood.

The cops. Ernie looked down at the dust and blood in the paper cup, along with the last melted bit of sherbet. He shivered.

It hadn't occurred to Ernie to call the cops. He had thought of calling Bert, obviously, but he wanted to feed Derek something first, to maybe try to make him more comfortable for a little while before his brother got there and started figuring things out, started making a problem out of the visit. Of course they should call the police, that would be the logical thing, wouldn't it? But Ernie knew, even before he went out to the front of parlor to where the white phone hung on the wall in order to telephone Bert, that they would never call the police.

Certainly they'd had encounters with the police since they left their life in the city. In fact the afternoon they took off, they stopped at the bank in order to clear out their account—a substantial bit of cash that they had to carry in more than one bag—and on the way out an officer was on his way in, and they passed each other at the front door. The man was shiny and blue in his uniform, with a little gold pin fashioned to look like handcuffs holding his tie in place. When he saw first Robert and then Henry with their almost matching polyester sport coats and same haircut and glasses, the officer stumbled a bit, a snag in his shiny, perfect presence. And the twins were used to this reaction, they got it all the time. But then when the officer swept his eyes over the men and caught sight of the matching bags they carried, money bags, he stopped in his tracks and said, "What's this then, bank robbing twins?" And he looked serious, the officer, his face grim and stern and his hand on his gun in its holster, but then he broke the spell by snorting and laughing and holding the door open for Robert and for Henry in his wake. "Have a good day, gentlemen," he said, still laughing some, and they nodded at the officer and walked—not too quickly—out to their Toyota and tossed the bags in the back seat and pulled carefully out of the parking lot.

And since then they always drove the speed limit and kept their license plates up to date and gave the local cops—the two deputies and the sheriff, hometown boys with associates' degrees and friends on the council—free ice cream when they stopped by in uniform or brought their kids in on a Saturday night.

Ernie let the phone ring eleven times like he always did, even though their rented house was tiny and it usually took no more than five rings to reach the phone in the kitchen, regardless of which room you were in. No answer, though, and he knew that Bert must be in the shower or way out back checking on his bonsai bushes, his nose full and his eyes streaming.

Ernie returned to the back room.

"You call the cops?" Derek asked, his eyes closed.

"Yes," Ernie lied. "There's some trouble out at Jack's Super, though," the fabrication grew easily. "Not sure what it is, maybe a real robbery. It's going to be a while." He picked up the grate from the floor and leaned it against the legs of the prep table and went about sweeping up the dust and bits of ceiling tile. It puffed up in little white clouds that made him sneeze.

"Bless you," Derek said, and opened his eyes. Ernie could feel him watching his movements. He used a dustpan to carry the debris to the big trashcan near the back door. Bert had left it unemptied the night before. Emptying the trash. That was one of Bert's jobs. Ernie shook off the twinge of irritation and turned back to his guest. Derek blinked upside down.

"You must be thirsty," Ernie said. Derek raised—or from this angle, lowered—his eyebrows. Ernie took it as a yes. Hours, he thought, the poor boy had been up there for hours, and now he just ate a couple of big scoops of ice cream which was filled with salt, everyone knew that, and of course he must be thirsty. Ernie was sorry he hadn't thought of it before.

He filled one of the large waxy paper cups with water from the prep sink and took a straw from a box. He climbed back up to Derek again, and lifted the straw past his eyes and nose to his mouth.

"Take it easy," Ernie said. "This could be tricky." But Derek, in that way that was becoming familiar to Ernie now, took too much of what was offered, gulped and choked and coughed, and Ernie had to duck his head to not get spit on. "What did I tell you?"

"Sorry, man. Sorry." Tears streamed down Derek's forehead into this hairline. His eyes were wet and wide and red. He coughed some more, craning his head away from Ernie's face. "Okay," Derek said finally, his voice quiet and rough. "Can we try that again?"

And so they did. And after some minutes of patience on the part of both men, the water was drunk and the cup set aside. Ernie got a soft terrycloth towel, one of those they used to wipe down the counter and tables, and pressed it gently against Derek's face, dabbing up the tears and water and snot left over from the coughing. The two men held eyes for what seemed like a full minute, and the gratitude that Ernie saw in Derek's gaze filled him like something warm. He folded the towel neatly before tossing it across the back room into the laundry bag next to the trash can, and stepped down from the stool.

Some time before Robert and Henry ran off, Henry had begun to see a girl. She was someone he had met in the laundry room of the apartment building, a chubby woman in her early twenties who had deep brown eyes and a soft smile. Weeks went by when the two of them always seemed to be there in the laundry room at the same time. No matter what day Henry did laundry (laundry was his job), the girl, Rachel, would show up in a matter of minutes after he did, carrying a white wicker basket of things, sometimes barely enough to make one load.

"Hello, stranger," she always said to Henry, even after the second time they'd bumped into one another, and she had reached out her hand and shook his with a remarkably firm grip and introduced herself. So they weren't really strangers and yet, Henry felt something like strange around her. Whenever they met he got itchy and tight at the back of his neck, and tongue-tied and hot in the face. Rachel didn't seem to notice though, carrying on most of the conversation by herself, talking about her cat and her roommate and her mother's bad knees and her job managing the office of a chiropractor in the Loop. She had a way of tossing her hair back from her forehead, a slight lift of a hand and a flip of her head, even though she wore her hair in very short coils that only bounced in place when she did this. The gesture made Henry's stomach clench in a small, pleasant way.

One day Henry watched as Rachel dropped two dishtowels, a washcloth, and one pillowcase into one of the machines.

"That all you got?" He said before he could think of any reason not to. "Barely worth the thirty cents, do you think?"

Rachel blushed a pink that spread under the freckles on her round cheeks.

"Busted," she said and turned to face Henry. Her lips, he noticed, were the color of plums. "I'm not really here for the laundry," she said and tossed her head and made her curls quiver. And after what seemed to Henry like an agonizing few seconds of silence and staring at one another, Rachel spoke again. "I live on this floor," she said slowly and nodded at him. It was like she was helping him figure out the answer on a quiz. "I hear everyone when they come down to the laundry room." She paused again and shifted her feet; Henry noticed that they were very small and she was wearing bright white sneakers and no socks. Her ankles, peeking out from the bottoms of her blue jeans, were tan. And then Henry got it.

"Oh," he said, and he felt as though he'd just awakened from a confusing dream.

They'd dated for what seemed like a long while before Henry and Robert had to leave. Movies each time, and they sat in the balcony and made out like the teenagers around them. Rachel was Henry's first real girlfriend since college, since their parents died and Henry, in his grief and love and fear felt attached to Robert in a way that took most of his breath, a way that left him little room for anything else. But Robert, easy, handsome, confident Robert, had had plenty of women, short intense flings that Henry witnessed through the walls of their apartment. Now, though, he could not get enough of Rachel: her lips on his; her tongue, tasting of salt and butter and chocolate peanuts, in his mouth; her cushy flesh under his fingertips; her hand rubbing down the front of his pants; her hot breath on his face when they came up for air. He wanted to go all the way, but he didn't know quite how to do that, and now in his twenties he felt too old, too embarrassed to ask anyone, least of all Robert who already teased him horribly in incredibly juvenile ways. "Henry's got a girlfriend, Henry's got a girlfriend," whenever Henry dressed for a date. And Henry ignored Robert except to see what he was wearing in order to put on something else—not the blue striped shirt like Robert had on, but the red plaid. Not the tan trousers, but the black ones. The oxblood loafers instead of the brown Hushpuppies. He never brought Rachel home; he never introduced her to his brother.

Henry suspected that Rachel would let him know when she was ready. That's how he thought of it, being ready, and he waited for clues in the things she did when they kissed at her front door (what would it be, he wondered, a tug on his belt, a slight lifting of her skirt, an invitation inside for a nightcap like in the movies they only saw a few of the opening minutes of?) Only Rachel always said good night at the door, mumbled something about her roommate and Henry's brother and slipped into her own apartment and sent Henry home to more of Robert's teasing and a cold shower.

And then things came apart.

"Hey," Derek said, "Which one are you anyway?"

Ernie used to like it when folks couldn't tell him and his brother apart. After all, Bert was the good-looking one, taller and more at ease with things than he would ever be. Bert's eyes were hazel, and in certain lights almost golden, while Ernie's were plain old brown. Ernie had a chipped tooth in front, a childhood leftover from when Bert threw a snowball at his face once, a snowball packed hard as ice and hurled with significant force when Ernie thought they were just playing, just messing around, and had lobbed only handfuls of powdery snow toward his brother's back. But when Ernie started to bawl and threatened to tell their dad, a stern man who was always embarrassed by Ernie's weaknesses, his girlish hands and skinny chest and easy crying, Bert talked him out of it like he could talk him into or out of everything. Like he had talked him into stealing from the company's accounts.

"I'm Bert," Ernie said; he didn't know why. Bert would never have fed Derek; he would have taken care of everything right away. Ernie wasn't sure how he would have done that, but ran through a series of possibilities in his mind. Maybe he would have gone ahead and cut the hole in the ceiling even wider, allowing the boy to fall into a heap on the floor. Or perhaps he would have pulled Derek free, ignoring his howls of pain as he twisted and turned the intruder's body in the air duct, working it and working it like a loose tooth, wiggling it from the roots, ignoring the hurt and the blood. But then what? Would he let the intruder go? Make him promise not to say anything, and they wouldn't either, Bert and Ernie, they wouldn't press charges so long as Derek kept quiet about everything, too. But Ernie knew, and Bert would know, that Derek, loud, boastful Derek, would have to tell someone and who knows what sort of attention that would bring to the ice cream parlor, to the twins, to their made-up, entwined lives in New Hope.

"Bert," the fellow said. "Bert and Ernie. Those really your real names?" He squinted at Ernie, his cheeks pulling down toward his eyes.

"Yes, certainly," Ernie said. He turned from Derek's inspection and busied himself with the things he needed to do to open the shop. He was already behind schedule. He'd have to do something about the smell that came from the air duct, metal and something else now, like some small animal might have died up there. And the tables needed to be wiped down (Bert never did this at closing time) and the sidewalk in front swept clean of the night's debris—cigarette butts, candy wrappers, bits of leaves. Once he'd found a single baby shoe resting against the curb, scuffed and laced tightly. Another time he found a pair of panties, teenage girl-sized and yellow, with the word "Tuesday" written in red script under the waistband. That was on a Friday.

Ernie pulled a sheath of napkins from one of the boxes and put it on the prep table. He excused himself and went out front to gather the metal napkin holders from the front counter where Bert had lined them up—empty or near—the night before.

"You're not the mean one, are you?" Derek said when he returned. Ernie pushed a handful of napkins into a holder.

"Mean one?" He said over his shoulder. "One of us is mean?" He tried to sound light, like this was a surprise to him, this opinion, like he hadn't ever thought of it before.

"Yeah. You're the nice one. You always give away free stuff, samples and shit." Ernie flinched at the word and Derek noticed. "Sorry, I meant stuff." Derek's words were beginning to sound slurred, like maybe he'd had too much to drink. "Samples and stuff," Derek continued. "And say someone's on a date, you know, trying to impress or girl or something, you know, in order to get a little...you know what I mean. And so you take this girl to the ice cream parlor, only it's about closing time. You're the one who lets us in, who lets us hang out a little while, lets us prime the pump with some ice cream, if you know what I mean." Ernie faced Derek then and saw him smile and wink, only from where he stood next to the prep table it looked like it was Derek's bottom eyelid that closed. "You forget about the pennies if we don't have them, you scoop heavy."

In fact, it was Bert who did all of the things that Derek spoke about; Bert who gave away samples and kept the shop open late and waved off the pennies and scooped heavy. Ernie made rules and followed rules, but Bert did things his own way. For instance, it was Bert who got to go all the way with Rachel years ago—or Robert, rather, not Bert—and Henry who didn't. Henry, Ernie, didn't blame Robert for that, really; after all it was Rachel who came over to the apartment when Henry was at the grocery store (shopping was Henry's job.) She was drunk from a party at the office, a celebration of the chiropractor's impending nuptials (Rachel had already invited Henry to come to the wedding as her date; he'd bought condoms just in case.) And how could Robert resist Rachel's mouth, her flesh, her tan ankles and warm, strong hands? It certainly wasn't Robert's fault that Rachel—at first— had mistaken him for his twin. Henry wondered when Rachel did catch on, did notice that Robert wasn't Henry at all but someone different, someone taller and handsomer and more experienced. When he got home with the bags of groceries and found Rachel crying on his couch, their (Robert's and Henry's) couch, and pulling the flaps of her cardigan around her body and Robert humming and scrambling eggs in the kitchen (cooking was Robert's job,) he was certain that Rachel knew who was whom, which was which. And when she looked up at Henry standing near the open door with his arms full of groceries, he stared back at her, dumbfounded and aching and queasy, unable to move or speak when she stood up and picked up her sensible navy blue pumps and ran past him and out the door.

People always got them confused. But Robert, Bert, was the friendly one. Which meant, according to Derek's description, that Henry, Ernie, was the mean one. This rattled Ernie—even though he always secretly suspected it—that people thought of him as the mean one. He was only following the rules. Keeping a certain order. There was comfort in order. He'd always felt it. It was one of the reasons he'd gone into bookkeeping years ago. All those columns and tiny squares on the pages of the ledgers, all the contained figures in his handsome, neat script. Since he was a child, he'd spend hours practicing writing numbers and letters in blocks, working to get the tops and bottoms lined up, the width of the characters uniform. It satisfied him. While Bert's homework assignments were scribbled in uneven lines and turned in on ripped and wrinkled paper, Ernie's were even black marks on bright white sheets. Perfect.

And yet, Bert always got better grades. Things came so easily to him.

Ernie forced another batch of napkins into a holder.

"Ernie's not mean," he said to Derek, his voice tight. "He's just careful. Cautious."

"Sorry, man, you're right. It's not my place. That's your brother, man. I get that." He closed his eyes again, and Ernie saw that his face had gone pale once more, the color of buttermilk. The dead animal smell was stronger. Ernie ran cold water over another clean towel and touched Derek's temples with it, then the back of his neck. "That's good, man," Derek said, his eyes still closed. "I owe you," he said. Up close like this, Ernie saw that Derek's skin was smooth, absolutely without lines, as though he'd never had to worry about anything in his life, never had to hold a difficult thought. In the mirror each morning Ernie studied his own face and the crooked grid of lines that now passed over it, new ones, it seemed, etched there every day. He rinsed the towel and used it to cool Derek's forehead.

"I'm sorry about that Jew crap," Derek said then, and Ernie pulled the towel away.

"Excuse me," he said.

"You remember," Derek said and he opened his eyes again, looked at Ernie. "Years ago. When you first opened up. We were just kids then. Stupid. You know. We didn't mean anything."

And Ernie's mind was blank for a few moments before it came back to him, that bright June morning when he and Bert arrived to open the shop together and found the windows painted with insults and threats and a backwards swastika. They were pretty sure it was the teenagers who did it, the boys who stood in line for ice cream and feigned big, loud sneezes into their fists: "Ah, ah, ah JEW!" And cracked up laughing. The twins had been in town for just months then, their bad deeds still fresh in the summer air around them. So when Robert said to get the bucket and the turpentine and forget about calling the cops, forget about what they saw and what they knew and what they imagined in the words on the glass, forget about everything, Henry agreed, pushed it out of his head, washed it away with a smelly rag and enough water to make it no longer visible, no longer there. This was something he could do, Henry, Ernie—he could make things neat. He could make it all clean.

"I don't remember," Ernie said.

"All right," Derek said. "I get that, too. But in case you do—remember I mean—remember that I'm sorry, okay?" Ernie went back to the sink and after a minute Derek said in a voice Ernie could barely hear over the water running, "What's up with the cops?"

"Yes," Ernie said, he poured bleach into the water and turned off the taps. "You're right. I'll go call again."

At the front of the shop, Ernie picked up the receiver and twirled the dial while holding down the metal cradle. He continued to hold it down while he spoke into the dead receiver: "Yes, this is Bert again, from the ice cream parlor. Yes. Yes, he's still here. Yes. Yes. Oh good. Thank you." And he noisily replaced the receiver in the cradle. "They're on their way," he called back toward the storage room. "Any time now. I'll be right back; I'm going outside for a minute." He listened for a response from Derek, but heard nothing. He pulled the push broom from its spot in a narrow cabinet next to the shake machine and unlocked the front door and stepped out into the spring warmth.

Close by, the door to the Temple of Air was propped open, and Ernie could hear the loud hum of voices spill out from it. He couldn't make out any specific words, but the sound reminded him of childhood and home, of Saturdays at the synagogue in the suburbs, a chorus of sounds aimed at something beyond knowing, at something greater than the everyday, something bigger and brighter and more beautiful than all that was visible. Ernie often stood silently outside the Temple of Air on a Saturday morning, listening and remembering and longing for something he could no longer name, something, he was certain, that was no longer available to him.

Once on a family vacation to visit their grandparents in Florida, the Saltzmans had gone to a Mexican restaurant in the lobby of a nearby hotel. It was the first time any of them had eaten Mexican food, and Grandfather Saltzman complained through the entire meal about the spices, his gall bladder, his impending need for an Alka-Seltzer. The food was too exotic for Henry as well, only he would never say as much for fear of disappointing his father who sat across the table with his face pinched up against the complaints from the older man. Robert, however, loved the stuff, doused it with extra hot salsa and washed it down with numerous Cokes. And after, the boys were allowed to join a dozen other kids on vacation in the tiled courtyard at the back of the restaurant, where they were blindfolded and given a stick to swing at a red, white, and green papier-mâché donkey until it busted wide open and spilled out squares of plastic-wrapped candy that tasted like cough drops and coconut.

The next morning Henry's grandmother wanted them all to go to synagogue together, but his father had made plans to go fishing instead. It hurt Henry to see Grandmother Saltzman's eyes moisten when they left the apartment in shorts and T-shirts, bound for the beach.

On the small motorboat (Henry had been expecting something else, a yacht maybe, like he'd seen in magazines at the dentist office) Robert began to feel ill, the night's overindulgence tumbling around inside of him as they bounced up and down on the waves. And Henry couldn't help it; when his father looked over at him, rolling his eyes in annoyance at Robert's moaning and heaving, Henry felt superior then, the stronger brother, the tougher, the better one. And when Henry caught his first-ever fish, a big thing, long and thick and silver-gilled and it flipped and slithered and thrashed at the bottom of the boat, Henry's father gave him a club, something that looked like a sawed-down baseball bat, and instructed him to hit the fish over the head, hard, and he did, tentatively at first, like he had the night before when he first swung at the *piñata* until he had slipped his blindfold up just a bit so he could see where to aim (he knew it was cheating, but no one noticed) and then swung harder. And the fish's head exploded, blood and scales everywhere, and Robert's face went absolutely white, except for where the bloody scales landed at the side of his nose and there wasn't even time for him, for Robert, to turn his head away, to vomit overboard into the sea. And Henry couldn't help it, he laughed at his brother covered in his own puke, and his father did, too. But then Henry helped Robert get cleaned up, throwing salty, cold water at him by the bucket, all the while picturing his grandmother later, home from synagogue and, once she saw this big, beautiful fish he'd killed for their dinner, willing to forgive him his truancy.

Ernie tested the weight of the push broom's handle as he swept the sidewalk. In another hour he'd have to open the shop. He wondered when Robert would arrive to work; he wondered if his brother felt better. On their childhood vacation, Robert had joined the family in eating Henry's fish; he had forgiven his brother for all those things he did and didn't do on the fishing trip. He knew that whatever happened, his brother meant him no harm. But life was complicated, and sometimes you did things in order to survive, and sometimes you did things just because you could. Sometimes you cheated and sometimes you stole. Sometimes you hurt people or insulted them for no apparent reason, and sometimes you were sorry, and sometimes you weren't. Sometimes you pretended to be who you really weren't or finally became who you really were.

Robert understood Henry like no one else did or ever would. They were almost the same man. Ernie knew this. Maybe that's why he had told Derek that he was Bert. He was Bert. And Bert was Ernie. He pushed the pile of cigarette butts and bits into the sewer next to the curb and felt the sun on his shoulders as he went back into the ice cream shop. The bell rang and the freezers hummed, but even as he neared the back room, Ernie didn't hear a thing from Derek.

Good, he thought. Good. He was tired of Derek's talking. In fact, he was tired of Derek altogether. He had things to do. He smelled the sharpness of the bleach in the sink. It was time now—the twin knew as he hoisted the broom to his shoulder—it was time now to get things done.

DEER STORY

And when you see it there on the side of the road (above it, really) it's already too late. You know. "Don't," you say. Out loud maybe. But it doesn't matter what you want (or don't) it's too late already, and it's hitting the ground on all fours then up again and into the lights, into the way but in the air still, bounding, and for a second you hope—maybe believe—it will clear. It will beat you, you hope, over that spot in the road, or rise high enough so you might pass underneath. But no. Of course not. You clip it as it springs up, feel the impact of all four ankles at once hit the front of the car, watch—foot hard on the brake where it's been since this started—as it lifts and tumbles, sideways up and over, an antler taking a stab at the top of the windshield, a road map of cracks spreading out and down the shatterproof glass. And it's behind you now. It fills the mirror, big and brown and coming down like something stuffed and heavy. You squeeze your eyes closed to absorb its landing, and when you look again it's gone. And that's when you swerve—too late, but it couldn't have mattered any earlier. (You find out from the handsome neighbor with the scarred wife that it's a path they all follow in rut like they are, third killed in a week in a quarter mile. Killed by the rut.) But still, you swerve, and ahead, the man you thought you loved but know that you will leave—in his own car driving home in tandem from a bar in the city—sees your lights weave out of his rearview then in again and then out as you pull to the side of the road and sit there, shaking. And his taillights flash white and he's backed his way to you, jumps out of his car and in shirt sleeves, with his hands jammed down his pockets, he bobs foot to foot outside your window. "What," he says and his breath is white shadow against black sky. He doesn't know. And you're mad that he hasn't noticed; it's just another thing he's missed. "A deer," you say when you open the window finally. "Stay there," he says then (for the first time. But not the last.) And you do this time while he runs around in the cold in the weeds, to his car and back, in the weeds again. For the smallest moment you think maybe, just maybe, it wasn't hurt, just tripped more or less over the hood of the car. But then the man you know you will leave comes back, his eyes bright in the dark and his hands trembling, holding—of all things—an X-acto knife. "This won't do," he says, "it's not enough." And you know exactly what he means. Then he tells you to go on home, get the neighbor to bring a gun. (The neighbor's a hunter you'd found out over burgers on the grill. They both—he and she—used to be. But his wife—nice woman, too bad about her face, one whole side scooped out from eye to chin—won't even eat meat now and hardly leaves the house.) So you do what you're told, drive on the last three miles alone, the windshield a kaleidoscope of darkness. You're crying now and it's hard to see, thank God it's a straight shot of highway. And in the nice little subdivision, suburbs in the country, split-levels and townhomes where the man you are leaving built you a brand new house (like maybe that'd be enough), you pull into your drive and run to the neighbors' and when you pound, he's there in a flash. And you notice again how handsome he is. You remember how his back felt when you rubbed against him, his whole self a warm wall between you and the cold air of the open refrigerator, his hands choking the necks of the beers, and you reached around him for yours, flattened your breasts to him, wanted him. And the man you are leaving was out there, with the burgers and the wife, but you were inside with the neighbor who turned around and smiled so small it looked like it hurt. Then he circled one icy hand under your shirt and let it get warm on the low curve of your back. And outside there was small talk and quiet, and inside there was nothing but this. But tonight his wife's there, too, in shadow behind him. It's always dark in their house, you can't help but notice. And they listen while you tell and he's half out the door when you remember this: "Got a gun?" You say and he stops dead, one hand on the doorknob, his face draining, white. And his wife steps back and turns away. But it's just a quick moment, a small shift, before he says "I got something." And he spins off in his truck and you make your way across the lawns to your house and inside and crawl into bed, clothes and all; and under the warmth of the blankets you shake and you pray. You don't even know if you believe in God, but shouldn't you apologize to someone? You didn't mean to do it, but you did it, and you asked to be forgiven, it wasn't your fault, but you were sorry, so sorry, so very, very sorry. And when your head was packed tight from the praying and the crying, you rolled onto your back—still, finally—and stared at the ceiling. You waited in the wide bed you shared with the man you are leaving, watched for the white columns of his headlights to come through the window. And then out of a dream starting, you hear voices, and the neighbor says somewhere outside the window "accident" and "shotgun" and "face" and "fault." And you put it together in the dark, about the neighbor's wife. The part that seemed missing. And you get it now, you've figured it all out. He did it. He'd shot half her face off (an accident, what else could it be?) yet still there they were. Together. And you hear the man you used to think you loved outside the window, too. "Oh my" and "Christ man, I'm really sorry," and his voice sounds different than you're used to, sounds soft and thick. But then they're laughing, the two of them, and the neighbor says, "We'd better gut this sucker," and you hear "Yeah, baby, fresh meat!" And whatever you'd started to think in that moment when his voice went soft, about changing your mind, about staying maybe, was gone. You hugged the blankets over your heart and turned your back to the window and knew in that way you knew when you'd hit the deer (there just isn't any other end to this story) it was already too late.

THE THINGS THAT'LL KEEP YOU ALIVE

It was at moments like this one—naked and dripping from the shower, leaning over the bedside table, rifling the drawer for a light—that I missed my breasts the most. That sounds odd, I know, but it's true. There's a definite body memory I have: the heavy swing of them, a slight tug from my shoulders all the way down to my rib cage. Only that's all it is, a memory. When I lean over now, the air is empty beneath me, and in some way that goes far beyond physical, I ache.

And maybe it's that ache that makes me stand back up again, and then not move even as I realize Arnold Huffner, Hoof, is there, right outside my window—checking some contracting matter, I suppose—and he sees me, exposed and scarred. He doesn't move, either, doesn't even flinch. His eyes travel down my neck to my belly button, travel side to side, following the scars. And it's like a whole day passes as we stand there, the warm breeze blowing in my window and bringing with it the sickeningly sweet smell from my mother's rose garden (neglected since her death), and the smell of earth and gasoline. Trucks pull up into my drive, I hear gravel spitting and men shouting and still I stand. And still Hoof stands. He looks up into my face, and I look into his, and his eyes are sober and kind like they always are, like they have been on those mornings when we share a cup of coffee before his crew gets there and don't talk much, just sit in an easy kind of quiet. Then he shrugs a little and turns back to whatever it was he'd been doing before this moment. And though I don't want to (what I really want is to lean out the open window and feel the cool sill against my breasts) I pull the shade.

In the mirror I saw what he saw. The stick-straight posture passed down from my mother; hair like rusty coils, wild and full and thick in spite of everything; a slightly worn, but perhaps not unpleasant, over-thirty face; strong shoulders; hips without much curve; flat stomach (thanks to the chemo); and the empty plane of skin stretched tight and stitched across my breast plate, my ribs. I sucked on a cigarette to light it, watched the chest expand and lift. When I got my first glimpse after the surgery, I'd expected there to be nipples. I felt them still, phantom nipples, and even though they'd told me all that would be gone ("There won't be much," said a perky A-cupped attendant, "but there won't be the bad stuff either") I'd expected to find them. Sometimes it happens like that still when I look in the mirror: where'd they go? I'd had nipples long before I had breasts; you'd think I might have them after.

This is how the day would go. I'd dress in the dark and listen to my house. Someone walked on the roof and it creaked. I'd move from room to room, stay out of the way, and listen. This small creak, a quiet groan, an occasional slam. All the changes the house was going through, I kept hoping it might make more of a fuss. But through all its years of us as a family here together, then the three short ones when my dad was sick, the long seventeen my mom spent here alone, the single one of her dying, and now this one with me back and trying to make it all it's never been—bright, big, open—this old house took on its own stubborn silence. The noise came from the work and the men who did it.

In the evenings, when the house was empty and quiet, I would go down to the kitchen, take the medicine out of the refrigerator, sit down at the table, unbutton my shorts and stick myself. I hated this part. I never knew what to expect, some times were better than others but always, at the very least, I felt nauseous. Whenever I gave myself a shot, I couldn't help but think about my friend Ariana who liked heroin "socially," she said, and how she said it made her sick each time she shot it, but then she'd vomit and then she'd wait a minute, maybe two, and then, miraculously, she'd feel like she was pure and golden, like she was magic.

So I'd empty the contents of the needle into my hip and put the works on the table. I'd look out into the night through my big, new, windows and wait (futilely, I knew) to feel like magic.

This time, it's a bad one. I'm going, going, going—all slipping down, down in the chair, down in my head, down deep and bad. I want to look out the windows, out into the cool black, but I can't keep my head up, it won't hold, and it falls back, rolls on my neck and it's the horrible bright white I see, the burning glow of the overhead fixture, big and smarting against my eyes. And I want to close them, close this out, this hot light, but I'm afraid, afraid if I do I'll go under, I've been there before, under the sickening spell of what's supposed to make me better. My stomach roils and my limbs loosen and I feel my forehead go slack and then my eyes roll back or close, I don't know which, but I'm not seeing my kitchen anymore, I'm in town, outside on the corner of something and Main, but I feel far, far away from everything, from everyone, and it's so dark now I can't see a damn thing, and the wind picks up, I can hear it, a great big whoosh like blood in my ears, and a tapping, and I can barely hold my ground, my arms are lifted from my sides and blow up and over my head like I'm flagging down a taxi with both hands high, but it's not me doing the lifting, it's the wind. And I know in a minute *I'm* going to lift off, to be blown away, up and over the houses I can't see but I know are there, out of the small town that for some reason I want more than ever to stay put in. And I feel a coldness creep up inside me, all the way from my feet up through my fingertips stretched and wiffling in the wind, and I'm afraid, terror-stricken and then, just like that, a hand is on my shoulder and it works its way up my arms and brings them back down and holds them, holds me. Not a hug or anything, just a hand on each wrist, and the dark starts to change, I can see things now, lights in windows and a shimmer of leaves on trees. And when I turn around, it's an old face I see, something familiar about it. *Don't I know you?* Maybe he can't hear me, the wind is so loud: whoosh, whoosh. He moves his head, a nod or a shake, I can't tell, and he says *You're okay, Sandy. You're all right.* And I shake my head hard, only I know I am barely moving and say *No* and I need to tell him that I am going to blow away. And he says it again, *You're all right,* and he's so close, I can feel his breath on my skin, *You just need some grounding*, he says, and he lifts his hand up and holds out two fingers and wraps my hand around them and says *Squeeze.* And I do, but I can't even feel my own grip, much less his fingers, and I search his face. *Are you sure I don't know you?* And the houses around us go dim through their windows and he says again, louder, *Squeeze, Sandy, squeeze,* and I hear it sharp and clear through the whooshing, and I do and I mean it this time, I squeeze as hard as I can, and I feel it up my forearm and into my biceps and all the way across both shoulders and down to my feet, which I can tell are on solid ground. And the lights in the houses around me go bright again, and brighter still, so bright my eyes sting—but it's a good sting this time—and the whooshing slows and goes quiet, and in the bright silence I come to and there's Hoof, his face familiar and close and his fingers wrapped tightly in my fist.

"You didn't answer when I knocked," he said when I dropped his hand. He turned away from me while I fiddled with the buttons of my shorts. "I saw the light, and it's pretty hard not to see right in here with all the windows." He faced me again. "You didn't look too good."

I nodded. "Uh, thanks," I said, trying out my voice. It sounded rough and too loud. "I mean," I said more quietly, "I mean, thanks. Thanks."

Hoof waved a hand between us. "Sorry to come by so late, but I wanted to share something with you." He walked back to the kitchen door, and I couldn't help but wonder, like I always did, why he tilted like that, heavy and stiff on one leg, pushing off with the other. He opened the screen and picked up his brief-case from the stoop.

"Hoof—" I started. Even though the worst of the side effects had passed I still felt shaky under the weight of the drugs. I wasn't up to looking at blue prints or tile samples or paint swatches.

The briefcase seemed heavy as he hoisted it onto the table. "Hoof," I said again, but before I had a chance to go on, he popped both clasps and flipped back the lid. The case exploded open and full of red, and it took me a second to realize that what he had there were tomatoes. A dozen at least, maybe more, big, red, shining tomatoes. "Jesus," I said.

"Damn straight," he said. "Grew 'em myself." And he picked one up and lobbed it—a slow underhand arc—in my direction and I caught the cool ball of it sure and true and bounced it in my palm, admiring its heft.

"Lovely," I said.

"Tastes even better," he said, and he selected another from the case and wiped it against his sleeve like he was polishing an apple and bit from it in just the same way. Juice and seeds ran down his chin. He smiled through the scarlet and talked through the pulp. "Fruit of the Goddamn earth. Here," and he pushed the glistening thing at me so quick and close that I didn't even have time to think before I opened my mouth and took it in, glorious and wet and sweet.

"Mmm, mmm," I said like someone in a commercial, only I meant it. And then I realized that I hadn't eaten since midmorning, hadn't even recognized I'd been hungry, because I'm not much anymore. But I swallowed down the mush and its coolness calmed the hot roiling in my belly, so I took the tomato from Hoof and finished it off in a few huge bites. "More?" he asked and I nodded and he pointed to the one I still held in my hand and I laughed and got to work on that one while he brought down a plate from the cupboard and sliced another tomato and twisted a pepper mill over it and placed it between us. We ate, concentrating and slurping, and I felt myself fill up in a way that I hadn't felt in months—maybe years—and each bite made me want more and more until I was stuffed and sighing. We sat back and groaned and rubbed our bellies. I patted Hoof's hand. "You're a good man, Arnold Huffner," I said. And maybe it was just the crimson afterglow of tomatoes, but I could swear the man blushed.

"I'm an old man," he said.

"Yeah? How old?"

He used the edge of the table to push himself up, "Water?" I nodded. He pulled two glasses out of the cupboard that he designed and supervised the building of. "I used to say 'Guess', but somewhere along the line people started guessing older instead of younger. Sort of got to hurting my feelings." He handed me my drink. "Fifty-five," he said.

My dad was fifty-five when he died, the cancer and its treatment had wrinkled and shrunken him. I was barely nineteen and thought that was what fifty-five looked like: brittle and gray. But Hoof was tan and healthy, burly and white-haired. "I'd have pegged you for younger," I said.

"You're kind," he said. "It's the job."

"Really? Contracting? I'd think it would wear you out."

He must have seen my eyes slide over his legs because he slapped the bad one and said, "What, this? This damn war wound?"

"You were in the war? Vietnam?"

Hoof laughed. "Nah." He thumped his chest with his knuckles. "Asthma. But I've seen combat. Hell, anybody's been married has seen combat. You ever been?"

I shook my head. "No. I got kind of close once, but then—" I thumped my own chest. Then I said, "I guess I've always been partial to being alone."

"Being married is as alone as it gets." And he shrugged a little, like he had that morning at my window.

"Jesus, Hoof," I dipped my fingers in my glass and flicked water at him, "Lighten up, will ya?" But I thought I knew what he meant. My parents had been married twenty-five years before my dad died. Most of the time they were in the same house they'd be at opposite ends; or if they were in the same room, they could be sitting side-by-side on the couch, not touching, not speaking, each reading a book or a magazine or maybe watching TV and, the way they looked from the outside, single and separate—my mom and her perfect posture, my dad hunched and gathered into himself—they might as well have been strangers in a waiting room. And then, after Dad's death, whenever I came to see her, I couldn't help but think how Mom looked and moved exactly the same way she had before. She took up exactly the same amount of space she always had, sat on her side of the couch, slept on her side of the bed, set her place in the same spot on the dining room table even when she ate alone. I don't know what I was expecting. Maybe that she would spread out some, reclaim the house as entirely her own. Or, since she didn't do that, maybe I thought she should look un-whole in some way, like parts of her had died with Dad. Maybe I wanted her to walk like Hoof walked, listing to one side, her body yearning for a support that was no longer there. Phantom support. But her posture stayed perfect as always.

"How long were you married?"

"Eighteen years."

"What happened?"

"She left me."

"How come?" I don't know why I wanted to know this, or even if I did. But the thing is, I had been alone in this house for six months (except for the men working) and, while I liked the solitude, I missed real conversation. Most times I talked to the workmen about nothing—answered the questions I could, made small talk about the weather, the headlines. When Ariana called, we were always interrupted by her other line or her pager, and it was hard to navigate a dialogue through that chaos.

"I drank too much. She screwed around."

"Because you drank too much?"

"Maybe I drank too much because she screwed around. I'm not sure now. Sort of a chicken and egg thing, I guess. I don't really feel like talking about it, though." Hoof rubbed his forehead with his palm, worked his thumb and fingers into his temples.

"Uh, sure," I said. "None of my business, anyway." And I tried not to sound disappointed, but I was never very good at that. I got up and pulled a fresh pack of cigarettes from the freezer, lit one up, set an ashtray on the table next to the empty needle. Hoof looked at me a good long time.

"All right, but just the short version." He took a deep breath, then: "Went out one afternoon with the guys after we completed a job way ahead of schedule. Got good and stiff. Now, I'm not too smart about what I can and can't do when I've been drinking, but I always knew not to drive. Paulie—you know Paulie? The good-looking young guy, my foreman—his first year on the crew, and he wasn't old enough to drink legally, even though we did slip him a couple of shots. Anyway, he's the most sober, so he gives me a lift, and I leave my truck at the bar. So now I'm home and watching TV and I hear this banging about on the roof. It's pretty windy that day, so I figure it must be some of those shingles I'd seen were starting to come a little loose. Anyway, drunk as I was—and I was drunk, let me make that clear—I climb up onto the roof and I'm not up there much time at all when Jackie comes home and it's windy, like I said, right?" I thought he wanted me to say something here, but before I could, Hoof went on. Fast. "So when she steps out of her car she looks Goddamn stunning, the wind blowing her long dark hair all around, she looks young and sexy and I'm thinking maybe I'll surprise her, you know, stand up and beat my chest like Tarzan up there on the roof, or maybe I'll do some flip off the gutter, land in front of her on the sidewalk, sweep her into my arms. You know, real hero stuff. But then this other car pulls up and it's some guy I've never seen before and she stops on the walk and he gets out of his car, and my throat tightens up but I'm thinking, okay, all right, nothing out of line so far, and they can't see me because I'm on my belly on the roof, and there's no reason for them to be looking up anyway." Hoof stopped and took another swallow of air and then drank the rest of his water, picked up a tomato and rolled it between his hands. He met my eyes for a second and then looked over my shoulder and out through the windows into the night. "So they walk up the walk, her leading the way and he's pretty close on her heels, and then he reaches out, slick as shit, and slides his hand over her ass and then up the back of her little skirt. And she doesn't even tilt." I wanted to tell him he didn't have to finish, but I kept quiet and kept listening and he kept on talking, and it seemed like our only option. "And then they're getting so close to the house I'm starting to lose my view, so I scrabble over the roof toward the edge—and I'm still stiff, remember—and the next thing I know, I'm on my back on the front lawn and Jackie and this asshole are looking down at me like I'm Goddamn Dorothy waking up after Oz."

"Shit," I said.

"Yeah." Hoof blinked a few times and made a sound that could have been a laugh. "Good story, huh? Anyway, she came to the hospital later—that's how I banged up my hip, in case you didn't already figure—and I told her to leave. And by the time I got home a couple days later, she had."

"I'm sorry," I said, stupid as that sounded. Hoof waved it off.

"I'm not. I didn't want her around feeling guilty—or worse, pity. Didn't want her confusing that feeling with something else. It wasn't until just then that I realized that she always loved me best when I was hurt. Jesus, not like that's healthy or anything, right?" He looked at me like I should say something here, take his side, maybe. Only all I could think of right then was how when I came out of surgery and saw Ariana there and a couple of other people from work, smiling and crying at the same time, I felt my empty chest swell up and heard my own voice in my head, small, quiet, young as a girl's: *they love me*, it said, and I knew it was true, *they love me.*

Hoof went on. "So anyway, you'd think this would be the time for me to really go off, you know? Get drunk and stay that way. But the thing is, I didn't. Once Jackie was gone, I didn't much want to drink anymore. I hadn't even realized until then how numb I'd been for so long. With her gone and the booze under control, I felt sort of alive again." Hoof picked up the needle. "Funny the things that'll keep you alive."

I stubbed out my cigarette, and without even thinking, lit up another.

"And those things will kill you."

"We're all dying, Hoof." I took a good long drag and blew the smoke in his direction.

"Now who should lighten up?" He said and swatted the smoke away, but then he added, "No offense."

"I'm thirty-seven," I said then, out of nowhere. Hoof nodded. I waited a minute before I said, "Okay. Now, you're supposed to say 'Thirty-seven? No way' or something here, Hoof." He nodded again and wiped his palms on the knees of his jeans and smiled that small smile, his eyes moved over my face.

"Looks like maybe you've seen some combat yourself," he said, almost a whisper. He took my hand and wrapped it around his fingers. "Even still, you're a beautiful woman."

And I tried to laugh, to lighten up, but instead what happened was I started to cry.

I'm not sure how it went then. Maybe he held me or maybe I held him. Maybe it was a kiss that started it all off, although who kissed whom is beyond me. But somehow it happened, and we ended up in my bedroom, my mom's room, really, on my big, soft, new bed and he's naked and I have my shorts off but my shirt on—I couldn't go that far yet and he didn't make me, this was as far as I'd been in almost a year and I kept thinking it should be more difficult than this, but it wasn't, it was easy—and he's on top of me and inside of me and his chest is fleshier than mine and hard, too. "What does it feel like, Hoof?" I can't help but ask.

"Warm, nice." He laughs a little. "Like I remember." And he pushes deeper into me.

"Not that," I say, and I put his hand up under my shirt on my flatness. "This."

He pulls back just far enough to look into my face. He runs his hand over my clavicle, my ribs, my scars. "Warm, nice," he says again.

"What else?" I take a deep breath and unbutton the shirt, slowly, slowly, watching his face all the while. He doesn't look away.

"Smooth, hard." He kisses that place where I remember the nipple, and, reflex I guess, I gasp and grind against him. He rubs his thick chest over mine. "Sort of like the first time." He moves with me.

"Like some flat-chested school girl?" I ask.

"No, not like that." He strokes my skin, traces the line of a scar with his fingers. "It's like how you imagine for a long time just what it will feel like, how wonderful and soft and electric, but still, that first time, it's not like anything you imagine." We rock together.

"Is that good?" The smell of my mother's rose garden mixes with the smell of his flesh, sunburn and Old Spice.

"Good, yes," he says.

I can barely hear him.

"So good," he says. Or maybe I do.

"So good. So, so, so good."

Ariana called from the trading floor, a slow day. "They miss you here," she said, and I knew it wasn't true, but I appreciated her saying it. "What's keeping you away from all this money?" She sounded giddy, her voice tight and high. I could tell she'd been winning.

"Come on out to the house," I said. "It's about done. The men will be around just a few more days."

"Men." And the way she said it, all thickness and breath, I couldn't help but remember the old days when after the markets closed we'd spend hours getting dressed up for the clubs, sucking in our cheeks and our stomachs in front of the mirror, making bets on who'd be wearing the same clothes to work the next day.

"Construction men," I clarified. I could hear the expanding sound of shouting on the floor. I looked at my watch. Twenty minutes to closing.

"Be out in the morning," Ariana said, and she hung up.

I knew better than to expect her in the morning; it was noon when the small, sleek, BMW pulled in the drive. From the wide windows in the kitchen, I could see Hoof's crew rest their sandwiches in their laps and their sodas at their sides and it was like a moment of stopped time when the door opened and Ariana stepped out of the car onto the gravel drive in her three-inch platforms, second-skin black capris and creamy white blouse. She tossed her short raven hair and smiled up the line of guys while she picked her way over the piles of lumber and scattered equipment that littered the path to my front door.

"Heaven, girl, it's like total heaven." And while she was looking around at the changes I'd made to the house—the new windows, the skylights, the bleached, highly glossed floors, the built-ins—I wondered if Ariana was talking about something else.

"Let's go out," I said, and I saw her face go dark, a quick pass, and then she grinned.

"Sure, sure," she said, "You're probably cooped up here most of the time, anyway, right? You change, and I'll wait outside." And before I could tell her I was already dressed, that shorts and one of my dad's old shirts I'd found in a trunk in the basement were pretty much standard uniform for me these days, Ariana went back out on to the front porch, tossed her hair, and lit up a cigarette. I'd seen this opening act before, many, many times. So instead of sticking around for the rest of the show, I went to find something else to wear.

I dug around in a box to find my pencil-legged jeans, the ones I used to have to wriggle into and then lie flat on the bed to zip. They bagged now in the butt and at the knees, and I cinched them up with a wide black leather belt that I poked a new hole in with a corkscrew. My stomach I knew was my best feature now, so I found a cropped tee shirt with puffy shoulder pads (way out of fashion) and hoped that my bare midriff and broad shoulders would draw attention away from the empty chest.

Outside, Ariana was talking with Paulie and Hoof, and when she leaned in close as one of them spoke, when she threw back her head and laughed, eyes closed, I knew what was coming next. The men let their gaze move down her neck to her breasts and Ariana knew it, too, and she'd work the moment—like I used to—shoulders back, chest out. And it Goddamn hurt me to watch.

"Let's go," I said, and took her arm.

"Where you women off to?" Hoof asked. It was good that he took his eyes off Ariana and put them on me then, on my face, on my belly, on my legs, on my face again. It was good that he kept them there.

"Get something to eat, maybe," I said. But I wasn't at all hungry.

"The Inn's got a good lunch special," Paulie said to Ariana, and I half expected him to ask to come along.

"Really?" And the way she said that one word, I knew she'd have left me to go with him, easy as that. It was an unwritten rule from the old days: better offer, no hard feelings. And for just a minute, I wished that it would happen. But then Hoof pulled Paulie back to work and Ariana pulled me into her little black car and we headed towards town.

When we got out at the municipal lot, I wished I'd worn my shorts. My legs felt weak beneath the heaviness of my jeans and my shirt clung to my back.

"We're here," I said and pulled open the heavy glass door to Anchors Inn. Ariana stepped past me and into the dark restaurant. I leaned back against the door and let its coolness work its way into my body. Slowly, my strength started to return.

"This place is famous for its ribs," I said as the hostess walked us to our table, "But it's got a pretty mean salad bar, too." Ariana looked around and I couldn't help but feel embarrassed by the tacky red-checked oilcloths on the table, by the fake, flickering, electric lanterns on the wall, by the red booths, their vinyl scarred with cigarette burns—and who knew what those yellowish stains were? "It's exactly the same as when I was a kid," I said. It sounded like an excuse.

Ariana smiled widely at me, "Very retro."

A couple was seated at the table next to our booth. They looked out of place, the man in fresh khakis and a forest green Polo shirt, the woman in a linen summer shift, simply cut, the color of eggshells. Once the hostess moved away, the woman reached for the man's hand across the table.

"An affair," Ariana mouthed to me.

The two focused so intently on one another they were unaware of us studying them.

"Maybe," I said.

Ariana lit up a cigarette and slid the pack to me. "So? Who's the guy?" She asked through a mouthful of smoke.

"Don't ask me," I said, still watching the couple.

"Not that guy, dope," she threw her lighter at me, "your guy."

"What guy?" I tried to stall, but we both knew it was no use. We had known each other since I'd moved to Chicago, a nineteen-year-old virgin. The morning after I'd had sex for the first time, Ariana bumped into me on the elevator at the Mercantile Exchange. "Your eyes," she'd said. "Yes?" I'd said. "You did it, didn't you? You can always tell from the eyes." And whether she knew from my eyes or from our big-mouthed desk clerk who had seen me the night before in the bar at Pago Pago with the man who would be my first, the bottom line was Ariana knew. Ariana always knew.

"It's one of those men hanging around your house, isn't it? Oh, see—you're blushing. I knew it—"

I dipped my head.

"Who? Wait, don't tell me, let's make it a game. I'll guess. If I get it, you buy."

And even before the game started I felt in my belly that it was a bad idea. But it was hard to deny Ariana her games.

"Good looking?"

I nodded.

"Strong?"

I nodded again.

"Wait, what am I saying—they're construction workers for God's sake. They're all strong."

I could see her walking down the line of men in her mind's eye. She ticked them off with a click of her tongue. "The dark guy's kind of cute, but too ethnic for you." She made a small ex in the air between us. "That boy, the young one?" She watched my eyes, I looked back at the couple. The woman was leaning forward now, speaking hard and quiet. The man leaned forward, too. "Nah, too much work with a young one like that. Not enough payoff—no matter what they say about recovery. A million quickies can't take the place of a good long screw, you ask me. So if it's not the young one—" I felt my shoulders tighten, my teeth clench. The man at the next table sat back now, crossed his arms over his chest, turned to look at something on the wall. The woman's hand stayed palm up on the table between them. "There is that old guy. Handsome, if you like that hard-ridden rugged look. But he's a bit damaged, isn't he?" Ariana went on talking, oblivious to what she had just said and to whom she had said it. I twisted my napkin in my lap. My head started to pound. "I mean, he's got that limp. Still, he is good looking. But old." She dragged on her cigarette. "Nope. Not the old guy. Not like he wouldn't be grateful. They are you know, those old guys, grateful for what they can get." She twirled her cigarette in the ashtray, sharpened the ember. "That's sort of a cliché anyway, isn't it? I mean, any one of them would be a cliché, the construction worker and the lonely lady in the house," she laughed and glanced back at the couple, oblivious, still. I think maybe I hated her. "Not the old guy, that would be like fucking your father."

"You're running out of options," I said, grateful the waitress was there to take our order. We passed the couple on our way to the salad bar. The man was speaking now, "…bad timing…I'm less than...please." The woman looked to be in pain, her lips pressed tight, her eyes squeezed closed.

At the lettuce, Ariana looked back over her shoulder toward the couple and snorted. "Oh, please, it's all so dramatic." But for some reason, I felt the tiniest knot forming in my throat.

"I know," Ariana said when we were back at the table. She pierced a cherry tomato with her fork. "The tall one."

"Tall one?"

"You know, dreamy guy. Oh, it is, it is. I can just feel it." She grabbed my wrist. "Don't tease me, it's him isn't it? The one with the dark, curly hair, nice ass. Come on, you know who I mean. Him."

I searched the crew in my head. "Paulie? You mean Paulie?"

"Paulie. Good name. Good solid, construction hunk name. And apparently he's not just a pretty face. I mean, you'd think he'd be sort of shallow, but—" and it was almost imperceptible when Ariana's gaze flicked down from my face to my T-shirt and back up. "Well, you know what I mean." Ariana lifted her white wine and looked at me over the glass. "Oh, you lucky, lucky girl," she said. I felt woozy.

Ariana started to work on her salad, satisfied with her choice. It didn't matter that I hadn't said yes or no. It was decided. The woman at the next table was talking again, only now she was crying, too, tears rolling down her face that she didn't even bother to wipe away. She sat back and tucked her chin into her chest. The man scooted his chair some, like he might move around the table to her, but instead he drank his water, spread butter on a roll. He started to speak, but then, he too started to cry. It hurt to watch, but I couldn't look away. And then they both just sat there, pulled apart from one another, quietly crying to themselves.

"Someone's getting dumped," Ariana said, and speared another tomato. And it was all I could do to not reach across the checkered tablecloth and slap her beautiful face.

By the time we got back it had clouded over and all but one of the trucks were gone. Paulie was there still, cleaning up scraps from the yard, covering materials with tarp. He told me that Hoof had gone into town for a bit, that he said he'd be back that evening.

"He left you here all by yourself, huh?" Ariana called through her window to Paulie. She put the car in reverse. "How convenient," she whispered to me and kissed the air next to my cheek. She revved her engine once, twice, and pulled off.

And then the rain came down fast and hard, and Paulie and I ran for cover. I left him on the porch while I checked the windows, grateful they were new so I could avoid my usual struggle with the one in my parents'—my—bedroom. I sat on the bed and watched the rain pummel the rose bushes outside the window. I thought about the last few weeks, about Hoof in this new bed with me. I considered what Ariana said. Hoof, a man as old as my father had been when he died. A kind man. An attractive man. An old man.

I thought of my parents in this room together, asleep with their backs turned against each other. I pictured my father in their bed alone, dying, and I recalled how my mother and I slept in one another's arms after the funeral, how I woke up in the middle of the night to my mom whimpering in her sleep, how I didn't know at first where I was, how I looked around the room until I recognized the paneled walls, the heavy oak furniture. I looked around again for my father, called out quietly, "Dad?" like I used to when I'd have a bad dream and he'd show up in my room and pat my head until I fell back asleep. Sometimes when I hurt myself, scraped a knee or banged my head, he'd just sit by me and hold my hand and tell me to breathe, "That's right," he'd say, "Breathe all the pain out." "Dad," I said again, lying there next to my mother that night, but then I remembered and filled up with such an ache, such a yearning, I had to lie flat on the floor and breathe the pain out of me. Or at least I had to try.

I followed Paulie into the bathroom because I figured if I was going to be a cliché, then this is the one I wanted to be.

"There's no leak—" he started to say, and turned around to where I was leaning back against the door, pushing it closed and tripping the lock without looking. "Ma'am" he said and I flinched at the old lady word, but in a second his face went from confusion to something else, understanding maybe; desire, I hoped. And I turned off the light and we were there under the sealed-tight skylight and the rain thrummed the glass and the gray sky gave light, just enough. And the two steps across the big bathroom's floor were giant steps—like in Mother May I, I thought for some reason—and then I was there in front of him and sliding down him, unzipping and releasing on the way, and I could tell he was surprised, but pleased, too, judging from everything. And he grew bigger and harder under my breath, my tongue. And as I worked the magic there, he tangled his fists in my hair (thank God I had that) and spoke low like a moan or maybe a growl:

"Oh," he said. "Oh."

And I was glad I was good at this, glad that I'd never been afraid like my mother had been. She'd told me toward the end of her life that she regretted that, never having tasted my father in that way, and after he died, never having another chance. "Things might have been different if…" she'd said. And her candidness surprised me and embarrassed me, and I changed the subject.

Paulie tastes good, salty and full and a little sweet, too, like I guess I knew he would, him being so young and all. Young and fresh. He smells of sawdust and hard work, and his smell warms me all the way through and then he says:

"What about you, baby? What about you?"

And with my mouth full like that, I can't answer, but what I'm thinking is how I got the only construction man in the world, probably, who wants to fuck when he can get sucked.

Then he says:

"I want you, baby. Let me feel you. Let me see you." And I'm grateful for that, so grateful, it's all I needed really, his desire. And he says it again, "Let me feel you." And it's like he means it even though his hands say what he really means, tangled up and pushing, holding me there, and for just an instant I consider pulling away and standing up and lifting my shirt and watching the complicated dark desire on his face fall away to something else like I'd seen before, that one time shortly after the surgery, before I moved back home, before I decided to be alone. "Take that," I'd say, "Take that." But he doesn't deserve that, being so nice to me like this, letting me have my way, so I just keep on and hang on his words—*I want you I want you I want you*. And for a little while, it's enough, this wanting, but he's a hard one and pretty soon my knees ache on the unforgiving tile and my jaw is dull with pain and I think, finish, damn you boy, finish. And then he does, a big, loud, juicy finish and I hold my place against his bucking and swallow it all, and when he stills, I rest on my heels and run the back of my hand across my mouth and look up through the mess of hair he made and smile.

"Oh my God," he says and he's beaming and hanging loose, the flat of his palms on the vanity behind him, the long muscles jumping and shaking in his arms. And he starts to laugh and reaches for me, but I tilt just out of his range and crawl to the shower—my knees screaming—and turn on the water. I push off the porcelain side of the tub and stand up slowly and say, "Undress." He's still willing, I can tell, his young cock already gathering strength again, and he pulls out of his T-shirt and kicks off his boots and in a moment of odd modesty folds his jockeys into the pocket of his jeans. He watches me the whole time. I pull back the shower door and wave him in and once he's closed in there I walk back across the bathroom (normal steps) and let myself out.

It was no surprise that Hoof was back when I came out of the bathroom, and even though I might have wanted it another way, I don't know, he just turned from me and went out to his truck and left me there and I stayed in my room until Paulie stopped knocking on my door, until he left me, too. I thought they might not come back, but they did, the next day and the next, courteous and cool, and they finished the job on time and finished it well. And Hoof mailed me the bill and I paid it in full, and it was months before I saw either of them again. I was working from home then, a computer in my kitchen so I could watch the market on the screen and the leaves go gold and red through all those big, new windows. Ariana came out for dinner and we went to Anchors Inn, and there leaning on his bum hip, one elbow on the bar, was Hoof. Paulie, too, and the rest of the crew. And I thought Hoof might be drinking again, like I thought—way back then—he might gather me up in his arms when he discovered what I'd done, like I thought he'd see that I was hurt, just hurt, and he'd forgive me and love me in spite of myself. But while the others held bottles of beer, he had a soda, and I'd be lying if I said I wasn't more than a little disappointed. He didn't see us and I haven't seen him since, and it was the last time, too, that I saw Ariana.

And now it's just me in the house, and it's bright and open like I wanted, but mostly it just feels big. I spend my days in the kitchen in my chair at the table, and my nights in the bedroom on my own side of the bed, and it's cool now so the windows stay closed and I can see the rose bushes shrinking and turning brittle.

Dripping from the shower, I stand at the mirror. My hair has grown some and my stomach is no longer flat. I light a cigarette and think again how I should quit smoking. Only I know

I never will. Some days I still feel the phantom nipples, and some days (not many) it looks like the scars might be fading. I take in smoke and hold it, my lungs as full as my chest will ever be. Sometimes you don't have much, I'm thinking—I release the smoke and squint and there I am, fuzzy and blurred—and what you do have is bad for you. But the thing is—I lift the cigarette and fill my chest again—it's something. At the very least, it is something.

THE TEMPLE OF AIR

When I saw Mom sneak a pack of HiDeeHo cupcakes out from the bottom of the pan cupboard and slip them in the pocket of her sky blue bathrobe, naturally I thought they were for me. It was my birthday after all, we were supposed to do that kind of thing for each other, right? Kind of like how I'd get up every morning and start the kettle for her hot water and lemon. Like how I'd turn the shower on for her fifteen minutes before I'd shake her awake so's the whole bathroom would be steamy hot for her. Little things like that. You know. Like a candle in a cupcake. No big deal. Just enough to show she cared.

I gave her time to get it together down the hall in her room, sat on the old blue couch and pretended to read one of the newspapers I'd swiped from school (Mom didn't believe in reading anymore, it weighed her down.) But when nothing happened—I mean nothing, no singing, no yelling, "Surprise!" or any of that—I decided to go see what was what. And when I got to Mom's room she was already dressed, her hair still wet and streaming water down the back of her blue cotton turtleneck, and there were no cupcakes to be seen anywhere. Not on her dresser, on her night table, in her hand or anywhere.

"Morning, Mom," I said, quiet like she likes me to be in the morning (she's not too good at waking up.) "Nice day." I stood with my back to the doorjamb, hands deep in my pockets. I tried to slide down and shrink up some because Mom was so teeny she always made me feel like a horse or something. Not like I was all that big. Just five-four and a bit over 110, pretty much average for fourteen (just turned.) But Mom was one of those bitty ladies, under five feet and featherweight, doll-sized, more or less.

"Hi, Baby," she said, still looking at her own self in the mirror on the back of her closet door, working a big, fat-toothed comb through the tangles in her blond hair. Mine's dark. Like Dad's. "Water ready, Rennie?" she said like she always did.

"Yeah." Like it ever wasn't.

"Put me some lemon in it, 'kay?" Like it was a special request.

But I didn't smart off or anything, I never did. I was about as good a kid as you could imagine. It was just easier that way. And I strolled down the hall like everything was normal to the kitchen and poured water into her blue cup with the shining gold letters "T-o-A" on it and tried not to let the lump in my throat that swelled around my wanting to hear something like "Happy Birthday, Baby"—or whatever—hurt me. And then it came to me while I was pouring. She probably was setting me up. Right that minute she was probably putting that candle in that silly little cake and maybe even pulling my present out of someplace at the back of her closet or the bottom of her drawer or wherever she hid things. So I took my time, squeezed an extra slice of lemon in the mug, and I pushed another down onto the cup's rim like they do in restaurants. I put it all on a plate with a spoon, stomped around extra loud on my way back to her room, gave her time and notice enough to keep the surprise a surprise.

"I'm back," I said, just before I turned into her room, but she was right where I'd left her, on that metal folding chair that was covered with a couple of pillow cases sewn together to look like some sort of slipcovers (which of course they didn't) in front of her mirror, still combing and combing through her stupid tangly hair.

"Took you a while," she said in that way she talked mostly now, sort of dreamy and soft. Like everything that took her attention only took it part way, like something else was going on in her head that didn't really have anything to do with what she was talking about. You know. Like when you're talking to someone and they're eavesdropping on a conversation behind you? They might be answering you, keeping up their part of the conversation and all, but what's going on between you is not what's uppermost on their list at that moment.

When I stepped over to the dresser to set the mug down, I guess you'd have to say I still had my hopes up. But next to the dresser there was Mom's little trashbasket she'd got at the Temple, the one the same sky blue as her mug (and chair covers and sheets and blankets and throw rugs and lampshades and pajamas and our couch and and and) and with the same gold "T-o-A" stenciled on its side and inside the thing was some Kleenex and stuff, and underneath that, I could see, was the empty cupcake holder. Pushed down under the other junk, hidden away. Like Mom does when she's been eating stuff she's not supposed to—hiding the evidence. And when I looked at Mom in the mirror, I could see the slightest trace of crumbs on her shirt, that shiny chocolate stuff that crumbles from the HiDeeHos no matter how careful you are to try to keep them from falling apart. And at that moment I was so ticked off and hot it was like steam filled my head. "You got crumbs," I said and pointed, and she said "What? What?" all shrill like she does whenever you say something like that, something about eating. It's the only time she ever seems to pay attention to the conversation, and that's just because she has to be on her guard to get her story straight, that story about not eating anything, nothing, surviving on air—Air Only—like they tell you you can at the Temple. But only if you are worthy, truly worthy, like the floaters and the High One himself, Sky (I kid you not, that's his name, Sky. The High One, Sky.) So most times Mom's pretending to survive just on air, and it's clear that she is doing that a good bit of the time as skinny as she is and spacey, but then there's those times she cheats, or Sins as they call it at the Temple. "Forgive us our Sins," they say, but usually they're just talking about eating, if you could imagine. Like feeding yourself, taking nourishment could ever, *ever,* be called a sin.

And then "I'm late!" she says, still shrill and jumps up and brushes a hand over her chest that used to have boobs, not big ones, but something more than that flat plane she's got now, and grabs her purse up (sky blue vinyl, like some old-lady Easter purse) and pushes past me and down the hall. And before I have time to say "Goodbye" or "Sorry" or "Hey, haven't you forgotten something—like the day I was born, maybe?" she's at the door and yelling back "Your father's here!" And I'm fighting to not cry, it's just a birthday, for God's sake, baby birthday shit, and hoping that maybe Dad's remembered, but knowing that will never happen, it's like some miracle he's remembered it's Saturday, our day, and that he's remembered his deal with the judge to do something with me, his only kid, his flesh and blood, one day a week, that he's remembered to come here at all. And I'm hoping as I tie the laces on my Nike Airs that maybe if he doesn't remember it's my birthday, I'll be able to forget too. And maybe then it won't hurt so bad.

"Where's your mom off to?" Dad asked when I stepped up into the cab of his jacked-high pickup.

"Church," I said, mostly because I was still mad and Mom hates it when I call it that. It's Temple or Service or even Worship.

"Again?" Dad said, and when I looked over in his direction I could see he hadn't shaved for a few days and his black hair wasn't combed and judging from his wrinkled up T-shirt and sweats he might have just rolled out of bed and jumped into the truck and come right over out of a dream. He smelled like beer.

We drove for a time, neither of us saying anything. It dawned on me that I was singing in my head: "Happy Birthday to Me, Happy Birthday to Me...." Then Dad said something, but I couldn't hear.

"What?"

"Fucking church shit!" He said and spit out the window. "Your fucking mom and that fucking church shit!"

Well it's probably clear to you by now that that pretty much sums up how I was feeling right then, too, but you know how it goes. You can say whatever you want to about your family to whoever you want to—you know, like "My sister is such a bitch," or "My grandfather is a perv," or "My dad is nothing but a drunk," and whoever you are talking to can even nod a little along with you as long as they don't actually say anything out loud. But no one else, no one else, can talk trash about your folks. Not even your own father.

"Shut up," I said without thinking. It just slipped out while I was still singing "Happy Birthday" in my head. I suppose I thought that I'd said it in my head, too, but I didn't. And as soon as they hit the air in front of me, those words, I imagined myself saying them into a big balloon like they do in comics and imagined myself reaching these hands up from out of my throat (heart hands, maybe, or soul hands) and pulling the string of the balloon back inside, the whole thing deflating its way back into me, and me swallowing it all down to my gut. And that entire little scene had to play out in just a millisecond because in the next moment Dad's hand was where the balloon had been in front of my mouth, and was closing in fast and smacking me—hard—across the teeth.

"Shut you up," he hissed, and that worked, because that's just what I did, I shut up and slid tight against the door and blinked and blinked and blinked the tears back (Baby, Big Birthday Baby) and decided right then I was not going to say another word to anyone all damn day. I ran my tongue over my smarting gums. Shut me up.

Of course, Dad hated that. See, he had that quick temper, but he also had that quick remorse some guys do, you know, a spanking followed by a hug. He needed you to tell him it's okay, you understood. So he was all soft-spoken then as we drove on down the highway past the old logging road that lead to the lake, past County Road G and GG.

"It's just that—" he started and put a hand out to my shoulder and I had to hold on tight to the handle of the door to keep from shrugging out from under him, "Your mother gets so confused. Well, you know that. And she is so gullible." And then he chuckled a bit, quiet, like he was remembering some little gullibility of Mom's from the past.

I didn't say a word.

"Like remember how she started selling that NewTriVision junk?" And he chuckled again, no doubt thinking about when I was around five and we were still all together in that little house in town (the brown one, all earthtones inside) and Mom had the whole front room stacked with boxes of NewTriVision powdered shakes and NewTriVision lo-cal cookies and NewTriVision tuna foodstuff or whatever it was in those little cans (the three— Tri—staples of the NewTriVision plan.) And every night Dad would come home wanting dinner and every night Mom would try to serve him up one of those "NewTri-cious and Delicious Complete Meal Replacement Drinks." I could still remember how he laughed the first time she tried that, dressed herself up in some white short-shorts and tank top and that white NewTriVision apron with the yellow triangles on it (the one all the Tri-ologists got just for signing up) and sat on Dad's lap on the brand new brown plaid couch and put the frosty mug of the stuff to his lips. And I can still remember how he pulled his head back, but not until his mustache was frothy with what was supposed to be vanilla shake but looked as fakey yellow as banana bubblegum and, well, not at all appetizing. And when Dad said, "What's this?" and licked the goop from his mustache and made a horrible tight face but kept his hands on Mom's tiny little waist and she said "Dinner," he threw back his head and howled. And it was clear from where I was—at their feet on the braid rug tracing the yellow letters on the NewTriVision boxes over with a magenta crayon—that Mom didn't like that Dad was laughing at her, and she put her head down and her lip out but Dad kissed her neck and pulled her close and said "Sorry Baby. I'm sorry—it's just that that's no meal for a working man is all." And she tried to tell him it was, "What with all the vitamins and minerals in it that fulfilled a hearty part of one's suggested daily requirements as determined by highly-trained New-tritionists." But Dad just laughed low while he went into the kitchen and pulled a Swanson's from the freezer and cooked it up for himself. And as the days went on like that, and the boxes stayed in the front room and Mom spent more and more time on the phone "recruiting," she called it, and Dad started working less and less with the weather turning cold and construction jobs finishing up, and dinner never getting made unless you were willing to try one of those fishy canned things or a shake (personally, I sort of went for the chocolate ones) well, Dad wasn't laughing so much anymore. And I can still remember when the fights started in the middle of the night, Dad talking low at first and Mom's voice starting out bright and tight and cheery like it was when she recruited. And then Dad would get mad and loud and yell about money and real work and Mom would babble about the miracle of success and the slow climb up the ladder and Dad would say "Ladder? What fucking ladder? It's a pyramid, Maddie, can't you see? It's a pyramid game—only they're illegal so they're doing this—"and here I'd hear him slap or kick one of the dusty old boxes—"instead!"

"But I'm on top, Ray, don't you get it?" Mom would say, her voice excited and filled with what I guess now I might call hope. But Dad would come right back with "On top? On *top*! There's only a top when there's a bottom. You got nothing, Maddie. Nothing. It's just you. Good old bottomless Maddie." And sometimes in my bed in my room listening, I'd giggle at that, because Mom was getting so skinny it meant something different to me than what Dad said. "But my prospects, Ray. My prospects," and usually about this time Mom's voice would crack a little and go soft and that always quieted Dad down, too, and this quiet talk hurt me more than all the rest of it because it seemed so thick with a sadness even then I guess I knew I'd get to feel soon enough. I was just a kid then, you've got to remember. And at this point in the arguments I'd squeeze my whole self into a little ball under my covers and stick my thumb in my mouth and rub my forefinger up and down, up and down the slope of my nose until it went numb. It wasn't long after that I'd be asleep.

We were getting close to town now, me and Dad, and my mouth didn't hurt anymore but I still hadn't said anything since he slapped me, and I could tell from the way he was squinting and working a hand over the leg of his jeans that he was getting sore.

"Remember?" he said again and of course I did, you know, but I wasn't talking. I rolled down my window. It was one of those summer-warm days, and the sky had that gold in it that it gets come fall. At the edge of town, the dry, stripped cornfields turned to trees with patches of red and yellow in the leaves. "And remember that—what was it?—Glamorous Miss crap that came next? 'Ray,' she'd say. 'You were right about that other stuff,'" and here he was making his voice all high and sing-songy like guys do when they pretend to talk like girls. I hate that voice.

But Dad was right. I even remember Mom saying that, "You were right about that other stuff," only not in the voice he was faking, but in her bright, tight, hope-filled voice. "*This* is it, Ray," she'd say. "*This* is it, Rennie," she'd say to me, too. And then she'd practice her pitch on the both of us, sell her way through the Miss Miracle Line. I'd bet she'd've been glad to sign us up, me even, a little kid who didn't have any money but what she gave me, and who was too young to wear the goo Glamorous Miss had her pushing. "Maddie, don't you see?" Dad would say when she'd start to draw her business plan on the big pad and easel Glam Miss gave to all its Glamourists—a triangular stack of empty squares where she'd fill in the names of her "down-line" as she "engaged" them. "Look, Maddie," Dad would say and push back his dining room chair knocking over a stack of crates marked GLASS FRAGILE, and Mom would gasp and put a hand over her mouth when Dad grabbed from her the complimentary pointer stick (silvery pink Glamorous Miss in cursive up its shaft) and traced the shape of her plan. "Pyramid, Maddie. PYR—" he ran the pink rubber tip up one side "—A—" then down the other "*MID!*" he'd swipe the stick across the bottom of the page, ripping it. And there was no telling who would storm out of there first, but soon it would be eight-year-old me by myself at the table wondering if there might still be some of that ice cream Mom had stuffed away in the back of the freezer behind the ice pack and freezer-burned rock solid roaster chicken. Mom had never gone back to real eating after NewTriVision introduced her to her New Thin Self, so there usually wasn't much in the house besides that. That and Dad's beer.

Dad was stepping on the brakes now that we'd passed the town limits sign and the SLOW 35 MPH posting. And as we cruised the avenue past the park, I could see the slumped shoulders of the usual kids, and Mary Ann's dyed orange head, I was pretty sure, and maybe Ricky's army jacket. But I couldn't have done anything with them anyway when I was with my dad, birthday or no. And then we were easing across the intersection of Main and Edison where the Temple was—just a storefront in a half-block long strip with Ernie and Bert's Ice Cream Shoppe and a dentist office and a daycare—and we couldn't help but see Mom's car out front. The big old Ford Fairmont—a leftover from who knows when—boxy and much too blue to go unnoticed next to the dusty pickups and wagons and compacts.

"So now it's church, huh?" Dad said sort of loud and narrowed his eyes before he pushed hard on the gas so his tires squealed. And he looked at me, raised his eyebrows up like "Well, got some insight here, smart girl?" But like I said, I wasn't talking. Only now it wasn't just out of principle, out of sticking to my secret pledge to shut me up. Now it also had to do with what I knew about the Temple of Air—Mom's church—and how it would really tick Dad off to know that this wasn't at all a different thing from those others (NewTriVision, Glamorous Miss, and the two or three more things Mom tried after he left) but instead it was painfully, horribly, exactly the same.

Like how you had to sell stuff to achieve a Higher Level. And while there was the usual junk—coffee mugs and T-shirts and bumper stickers (Air Head—I swear to God—Aboard) all sky blue and marked with the gold "T-o-A"—the High One, Sky, wanted more. He had bigger ideas. He figured they could sell everything that had anything even remotely to do with air. So as you'd expect, there was air freshener and balloons and kites and wind chimes and air socks and fans—even some old-fashioned gliders made out of that wood that's lighter than a popsicle stick. And then there was the other stuff: blow-dryers, vacuum cleaner bags and, no kidding, whoopie cushions. Now to me those last things were a stretch—and (maybe it's just me) sort of, well, disrespectful.

"I hear rumors those people are supposed to be able to fly," Dad said. We were pulling into Jack's Super, so I knew he was going for beer and cigarettes, which meant we'd probably go back to his place where he'd smoke and drink and jump from channel to channel with his universal remote control. Some birthday.

I looked at him.

"Hear me?" Dad asked. "I said, I hear rumors they're supposed to be flying in there."

Floating, I wanted to tell him, they call it floating. But now I was too deep into this shut-me-up stuff, so I kept it zipped.

"What, you believe this shit?" Of course I didn't. What'd he think I was, some goof? But I wasn't talking. And even if I was, I wasn't sure I'd tell him what I knew. How each member starts on the ground—earthbound, they call it. And how by selling all that junk and bringing in new members and not eating and probably some other weird this and that, you got a little higher and higher off the ground. Mostly it's figurative, this off-the-ground thing, but supposedly, those who are truly worthy—well, like Dad said, there are rumors. But he wasn't going to hear it from me.

Dad put the truck in park and faced me. I stared at him. "Do you believe this shit? This flying shit?" He waited for me to answer, which, you already know, I wasn't doing. "Huh? Huh?"

Now I'm not a fool, I knew what was coming. But even if I started talking now, it wouldn't have made any difference. You know. So why bother? I just grabbed hold of the door handle like I did when he took me four-wheeling and I held on for the ride. "You believe this shit?" And then it was like an explosion, the cab of the truck filled with his hollering. "Fine. You believe it. You just fucking believe it." And he balled up his fists on his thighs. "You and your mom. Exactly the same. Fine. How about it? Would you rather be with her right now? Want to be with her at that—that—church?" He started to sputter, and I just kept my grip on the handle and watched his whole body shake. "You want to go with her? Fly around? Do you? Do you?" His face was close to mine now, and the beer smell was right there on his skin, like he was sweating the stuff. His eyes, right up in front of my own, looked electric and shut off at the same time. How did he do that? And then he reached behind me for the handle, slapped my hands off it and pulled it up. "Go. Get the fuck out of here. You want to fly? You fly! Fly away, chicky!" I nearly fell out of the big old truck, but I got a foot down first to right myself. I sure didn't want anyone to see me on my ass on the cracked cement of the Super lot. On my ass on my birthday. And then Dad was squealing tires out of the place, the door hanging open and flapping on the side of the cab until the truck turned hard back onto Main and it slammed itself closed.

Fine.

He'd be back. I wasn't worried. He always came back. But this time, I'd be gone.

I somehow ended up at the little brown house. A big hand-lettered sign stuck in the patchy front yard read FOR RENT, and underneath in smaller letters, *furnished*, and, *like new*. Around back was an alley I used to ride my bike up and down. The earth-colored couch, the one Mom and Dad and I used to sit on to watch "Family Ties" together stood upended against the garage. The cushions, worn through so the stuffing popped out of their centers, were stacked in a sad little pile. And seeing it all there, our house empty and our furniture garbage (sure it had been three years since we lived there, and we were just renters, but still—) well, it was more than I could take. I put my butt down on that little pile of pillows, sunk close to the ground, and thought about crying. Big Birthday Baby.

Well, you know how it goes. Crying and feeling sorry for yourself only works for a little while, and once I'd had enough of it, I had to figure out the trick of getting home. No way was I going to Dad's. I liked the idea of him rolling back into Jack's— all slow and sorry—and not finding me there. Maybe going in and asking at the counter, maybe knocking on the Ladies' Room door. And then cruising the avenue, under the speed limit and watchful. Getting scared maybe. Especially when he'd pull into the park—sure that he'd find me there—and no one would've seen me. That'd teach him.

I decided to go to the Temple and wait Mom out in the parking lot. It was just a couple of blocks, but I kept to the alleys and side streets so there'd be no chance of running into Dad.

"Can you see anything?"

The voice, out of the clear blue like that, made me jump. I whirled around from where I was trying to see through the Temple's front window.

"Are they flying?"

He was less than a foot from me. I don't know how he got there without my hearing, but there he was. I knew this guy. Everyone in town did. Well, knew of him, I mean. He was the homeless guy. That's what we called him. No one I knew knew his real name, and he was the only person who was homeless in town. The Homeless Guy. Only, up close, he didn't look how you'd expect a homeless guy to look. Sure his hair was long and he had a raggedy beard and jeans and a shirt all worn through in those spots that go first—knees, elbows, butt—but from where I stood he looked clean and, well, as far as I could tell, sane. Like he stood up tall and wasn't talking to himself and wasn't scratching or squinting or whatever you might expect some crazy homeless guy to be doing.

"Michael," he said and held out a hand to me. A surprisingly clean hand.

The way I saw it, I had a couple of options here. I could keep on not talking, ignore the guy. But that would be rude, and my mom didn't raise me to be rude. And I wasn't mad at this guy—heck, since I'd sat down and had that cry, I wasn't really mad much at all anymore. So it didn't seem quite right to take things out on this Michael. So, "Hi," I said, taking the second option, the talking one, "I'm Rennie." But I kept my hands to myself. I figured I was just fourteen; it was okay if I wasn't into shaking hands.

"Did you see them fly?" Michael stepped in front of me and put his eye up against the window where I'd been looking through. There was a little space between the blue curtain and the wall inside, but the angle wasn't right. All you could see was the edge of a blackboard or something. "There's a better place to watch from," he said, his head still pressed up against the glass. His words made a circle of steam on it. "Wanna see?"

I really just wanted to go home. But I was pretty much stuck. I wasn't allowed in the Temple, Mom had made that clear the last time I went with her a couple of months ago and made the mistake of asking if it would be all right to have one of the candy bars she always kept in her purse. You'd think I'd asked for a joint or a gun or something the way the whole "congregation" gasped and tsked. Mom got so red I thought she'd pop. And so here I was stuck outside waiting for her and the Temple was open for another hour. And Mom never, ever left Temple early.

"Sure," I said to the guy and shrugged just enough to show him how much I didn't really care. "Let's see."

And then the thing is, I was following this guy who didn't really look crazy like I said, but who I had pretty much come to believe was crazy ever since I first saw him right here, in front of the Temple, sleeping in the doorway some months ago. And even though he didn't look like what I expected (damn TV shows, give you all sorts of wrong ideas) he still wasn't anyone I knew or should trust. And at first I had all those thoughts you get, you know—he's gonna kill me, or he's gonna rape me, or he's gonna mug me—and in that order, starting with the worst and then getting less and less serious. But there was something about this guy. Something quiet. Quiet, but intense. It might have been scary, this way he was, like if you met him in some back alley or someplace dark and deserted maybe. But as we went around the side of the building, past the daycare and behind the place, in all this broad daylight, I wasn't scared at all after a while. We climbed up onto a crate, then up onto the top of a dumpster, then he reached high and grabbed hold of the wall that edged the roof and used a doorframe to step up and over. He held a hand down to me and finally I got the doorframe under my foot and was up and over and onto the roof next to him. Then he turned his back on me and started fast across the roof, the tails of his shirt flapping behind him. I followed, slower though, my hands deep in my pockets.

And you know what? Up high like that, I have to admit, things looked pretty good. The tops of the trees were bright with those leaves turning red, turning yellow and orange. You could see all the way down Main Street to where the highway came in, and the fields beyond town tilted up with the rise of the land. Shimmering, it looked like from up there.

"Here," Michael said waving me in. He fell to his knees and pushed his face against the roof. I kneeled next to him. He smelled like the woods around the lake. Like fresh air and damp earth. "Yup," he said and moved a little to the side so I could get a look. "There's old Sky himself." I was surprised that he knew the High One's name, but I guess it's sort of like how I knew he was The Homeless Guy. In a town this small, everyone knew everyone who wasn't one of the regulars.

I looked through the crack, just a small opening, but big enough to see through with one eye. And the place was exactly as I remembered it, pale blue and empty pretty much, except for a couple of bulletin boards and blue blackboards and the display case where they kept the smaller things they sold. The only thing different was that the chairs were out of the way, folded up and pushed off to the sides, and the floor was covered with mats. Big, lumpy mats, like they had in the wrestling room at school. Blue mats.

I saw my mom. I recognized the top of her head, although I'm not entirely sure how since I don't know that I ever looked at it before—but I did. She sat in the middle of the mat, her legs crossed over in that way people do—swamis and stuff—the feet on top of the knees. I didn't know she could do that. And there was Sky, skinny as a reed, in front of her on the mat, sitting the same way. Even from up here I could see how tan he was, especially in his blue robey thing, and I thought like I did whenever I saw him that it was funny how he always looked sort of windswept. His bright blond hair flew back away from his face—from using the official Temple blow-dryers, no doubt. They were knees-to-knees, Mom and Sky, no one else was there. They sat absolutely still.

"Are they flying?" Michael asked. If someone else asked me this question, I'd pretty much have to think they were joking. Flying. Right. But Michael sounded really sincere. Not like he was making fun or anything. Like he really wanted to know. Like it could ever be possible.

"No," I said, keeping watch. The two beneath me didn't move. I tilted my head a little so I could use the other eye for a while. But nothing happened. They sat and I sat watching.

I don't know how long I had my eye pressed against that crack waiting for something to happen (which never did) but when I sat back up, rolled the kinks out of my neck and looked around, Michael was gone.

Back on solid ground again I went into Ernie and Bert's. The place was empty except for one of the old twins, Ernie, I think, or maybe Bert. And in that place that never changed (tinny door chimes, eight-panel menu board, white plastic tables and chairs, red trim at the tops and bottoms of the bright white walls) I couldn't help but remember when I was five, the first time we came here, Mom, Dad and me, on my birthday—back when Mom would still eat in public. "Whatever you want," Dad had said as he lifted me up so I could see into the big tubs. Twenty-three regular flavors and four monthly specials. Millions of possible combinations. "Whatever I want," I said to myself after I let go of the memory, and ordered the biggest thing they had: triple banana split, whipped cream, nuts and cherries. Why shouldn't I?

At the front table by the window, I dug in. When I stopped eating long enough to get a breath, I looked up and there was Michael—outside looking in. I waved to him, and I guess he took that to mean come on in, because that's what he did. The chimes banged on the door as he passed through, then he came over and plopped into the little white plastic chair across from me.

"Looks good," he said, "Special treat?"

"Yeah," I said. I was half-way through the middle scoop (rocky road) and working my way toward the rainbow sherbet. "It's my birthday," I said. And it was sort of like letting loose a secret you've been dying to tell. Once I said it I was glad I'd said it, but a little—oh, I don't know—ashamed, I guess.

"Yeah, well, happy birthday," Michael said.

"Thanks," I said, and looked at him. He had an okay face. One of those smooth ones that makes it hard to tell how old a person is, but I figured him for thirty or so. Maybe forty. He had bright blue eyes, kind of gold, too, like the autumn sky. Or maybe it was just a reflection. He stared at my banana split, followed the spoon from the banana boat to my mouth and back with those eyes. It got to be kind of hard to keep eating, him watching me like that, so I put the spoon down and tried to come up with something to say. I looked out the window at Mom's big blue car, then over at the plate glass front of the Temple.

"You know Sky?" I asked.

"Used to," Michael said. He kept his eyes on the ice cream.

"When was that?"

"Back as kids. Long time ago. But we parted ways." He scratched a spot on his nose and looked up. "You, uh, gonna finish that?"

Well, I wanted to. Bad. But it didn't seem quite right then, so I shook my head and pushed the banana boat across the tabletop toward him. He reached for my spoon and scooped up a mound of the stuff. I watched him for a bit. It was like there was barely time for one spoonful to melt in his mouth before he shoved another one in there.

"Parted ways how?" I asked when he stopped long enough to wipe his mouth with the back of his hand. "I mean, besides the obvious."

"Obvious?"

"Yeah, you know. The eating. You guys clearly have different ideas about eating."

"That so?" He closed his mouth around a spoon of rainbow. He went back to work on the banana split without answering my question. I tried again.

"Were you ever a member of the Temple?"

Michael just snorted. Green and pink sherbet spotted the edges of his mustache.

"But you know about the floating."

Michael shrugged and picked up the boat with both hands and licked the inside clean. Then he slid it aside, tilted his head slightly. Behind him I could see Ernie working a towel over the counter, cleaning like he always did.

I didn't say anything for a bit, and neither did Michael. I don't think he intended to do much talking. So I went on. "Do you know how that floating stuff goes?" Michael shook his head. "I do. I've seen it."

"Yeah?"

"Yeah. Supposedly Sky is the one who can really float. You know, truly worthy and all. And a couple of the others sort of can." I figured he must know this, but he let me keep talking. "It's not floating, though" I said. "It's jumping." Michael leaned across the table, watched my mouth as I spoke. I couldn't help but lean back a bit. "Seriously. They sit like we just saw them sitting," I pointed my thumb out toward the parking lot, "and then they gather up all this energy, and jump. They keep their legs crossed, so it doesn't quite look like jumping. But that's what they're doing. Only they're so full of themselves and so dizzy from not eating they think they're levitating. A few inches off the ground and a couple feet covered. Big whip. You ask me, that's not floating."

"What about Sky?" Michael says in a polite way, like he's taking part in the conversation just to be nice, like maybe I'm not telling him anything he doesn't already know.

"Same thing. Only he's really good at it. He rises up pretty high and goes a pretty long way. To me it's like he's the champion of the cross-legged long jump. And whenever he does it—and he rarely does, you know, to keep the mystery going—everyone starts sighing and gets all quiet. Like they've just witnessed the second coming or whatever. Like it's a Goddamn miracle."

Michael's staring hard at me now, his sky eyes locked with mine. I've got to look away. "No such thing as a miracle," I say.

And that's when I hear the squeal of tires in the parking lot behind us, and I know even before I look that it's my dad. And when I do look, there's Mom, too, coming out of the Temple doorway. She sees Dad's truck first, and I can't help but notice how she reaches a hand up to her hair and smoothes it down, how she puts her shoulders back and holds her head high—like she used to when she heard him come into the door of the little brown house: "Honey? I'm home!" And I notice, too, through the dusty windshield of his truck, how Dad smiles first when he sees Mom, and then how he runs a hand over his face and pulls the smile off. And how when Mom sees him do this, she frowns, too. And I know I've got to get out there before it really hits the fan, and I jump up quick and hold out a hand to Michael which he shakes.

"See ya," I say.

"Yup," he says.

I dash to the door and pull it open, and here's where things get weird. The chimes that have been ringing in that place for as long as I can remember sound different then. Brighter and, well, sort of magical.

"Rennie," Michael says, and I turn to see him stand. Funny thing is, he's much taller than I remember, his head rising closer and closer to the ceiling. And then his feet are hovering over the tabletop, and I follow the line of his legs up past the holes in the knees of his jeans, let my eyes make their way to his.

"Happy Birthday to you, Rennie," he says. And I quick look around to see if Ernie's seeing this, too, but his head is down in the freezer case, attending to some cleaning matter. And I look back toward the parking lot to see if maybe Mom and Dad—but they're standing face to face and talking, not yelling or anything, just talking. And I look again and Michael's still up there, floating and floating and floating. He smiles at me, and nods. "There you go," he says, and then I nod, because the way I see it, that's pretty much all there is for me to do.

And so I step out onto the sidewalk and start to cross the parking lot toward Mom and Dad and they turn and see me, and they both get that look of relief only parents can have at those times when they know their kid is safe from whatever. And I'm thinking maybe my folks will remember now, maybe we'll go out and celebrate or something, I mean it is still my birthday, right? But then the look starts to turn a little gray on each of their faces, and I know what to expect next. I glance back over my shoulder and into Ernie and Bert's, and it's just Ernie in there now, clearing the table, throwing away my empty. And then up ahead I see Dad reaching for his belt and Mom's eyes go blank and spacey.

So that's when I do it. Float, I mean. I just swallow and swallow and fill up with air and close my eyes and rise. I rise up and out of this here, up and out of this now. I lift and lift, higher and higher, over the tops of their heads, over the tops of the trees starting to die, over the top of the Goddamn Temple of Air. Over and over and over it all. I'm floating, damnit. I'm floating.

Acknowledgements

Much gratitude to the journals and anthologies that published versions of these stories along the way:

F Magazine, "Something Like Faith;"
Superstition Review, "Just Like That;"
Fish Stories Collective 3 and *Criminal Class Review*, "The Joke;"
Dunes Review, "Running;"
Dogwood, "When is a Door Not a Door?;"
Sleepwalk Magazine, "Hand Thing;"
The Thing About Second Chances Is...(Polyphony Press) and *Coe Review*, "The Way it Really Went;"
The Thing About Hope Is...(Pearson), "Deer Story;"
Other Voices, "The Things That Will Keep You Alive;"
American Fiction 10: Best Unpublished Stories by Emerging Writers (New Rivers Press) and *Slow Trains* (Samba Mountain Press), "The Temple of Air."

Much gratitude, too, to the institutions and organizations that provided financial and moral support, as well as gifts of space, time, grants, and awards:

The Illinois Arts Council; Vermont Studio Center; Glen Arbor Arts Association; Interlochen Arts Academy and College for Creative Arts; Bath Spa University; Elephant Rock Productions; The Sabbatical and Faculty Development Committees of Columbia College Chicago; and especially, The Fiction Writing Department of Columbia College Chicago.

THE TEMPLE OF AIR

P A T R I C I A   A N N   M C N A I R

A Reader's Guide

A Conversation with Patricia Ann McNair

Elephant Rock Book editor Dan Prazer visited Patricia Ann McNair in her office at Columbia College to discuss the process of writing *The Temple of Air*. Find more about Patricia at patriciaannmcnair.com.

Dan Prazer: What was your starting point for *The Temple of Air*?

Patricia Ann McNair: I wanted to write about this place, a place that became New Hope. It's a loose composite of Mount Vernon, Iowa, where I went to school, and Solon, Iowa, where I lived for a while, and Mount Carroll, Illinois, which is a small town where I have a house now, and upper northern Michigan. All of these places, to me, are very much Midwestern, but at the same time, very rolling and very woody. A lot of people think of the Midwest as Nebraska, flat plains, and I wanted to challenge that perception somewhat.

I also very much wanted to write about faith, religion, magic and superstition. What can we believe? What matters to us? What is at the helm? I mean for a number of these stories to be, for lack of a better word, spiritual, full of faith, but not blinded by it.

The story "The Temple of Air" came to me when I was watching a bad cable show about magicians and this one guy, this hip new magician actually floated. He lifted himself up a few feet in the air on a New York City street. There was a girl in the show who was watching him, and she totally freaked out. She started shaking and squealing and said something like, "It's my birthday, and I saw a man float." Something about that combination of words stuck with me. I also happen to be a bit of a birthday baby, so these things, observation and emotion, came together for me. In the story there's a girl who sees something (or perhaps doesn't see something) similar on her own birthday.

There's a relationship mentioned between a couple of characters, Michael and Sky, toward the end of that story. As I was writing that story, I knew—in that way writers seem to know things about their characters—that they'd been friends a long time ago, but aren't friends anymore. It took me about a year to figure out what their friendship was a long time ago and how they had separated. And that's when the first story, "Something Like Faith," came to me.

"Something Like Faith" was inspired from something I witnessed while riding on the big Navy Pier Ferris wheel in Chicago. These parents were just letting their kid run around the gondola as we were going in this huge circle high above Lake Michigan and Navy Pier. It made me queasy to even watch. It made the ride so incredibly unpleasant for me, and I couldn't get the idea out of my head — what would happen if this kid fell? I had to write it out to find out what would happen, and how this tragic event might affect its witnesses.

Once I finished SLF, I had the first story and the last of the collection.

DP: Is that useful to you as a writer, to know the bookends in order to fill in the middle?

PAM: I think once I figured out that this was the inciting chapter, for lack of a better word, and that the other was the ending chapter, then the rest began to fall into place. So it became useful to me the more I wrote and explored. Only it took me a while; I didn't immediately recognize it as a place to start putting together the collection. I am not certain I knew I was working on a collection in the beginning. I was just writing stories that pulled at me.

I think we write a lot of things by accident. In the story "The Way It Really Went," there is a section where the couple is in bed and the husband starts to have these dreams and the wife cuddles up to him. That was just an exploration in a journal, and I was sitting in on a class with (Fiction Writing Department Chair) Randy Albers just to keep the writing going in my first semester of teaching full-time at Columbia College Chicago. And I read the journal entry out loud but said, "This is just an exploration. This isn't going to be part of the piece," and somebody in that class, who is now also a faculty member, said, "What the hell are you talking about? It's got to be in the piece." I don't know that I would have figured that out without somebody telling me. Maybe I would have, but it probably would have taken me longer.

DP: It sounds like journaling is an integral part of your creative process.

PAM: I use my journal a lot to discover various parts of story, and it has happened more than once that I've written something then forgotten about it, only to find it later and put it to good use. Sort of like when you drop your jigsaw puzzle pieces on the floor, and try to put it all together but there's still this hole. In frustration you start searching, turning over cushions and looking under things. Then you move the couch, and there it is, the piece that had gone missing. And now you can fill the hole.

DP: I was struck by the relationship between Sky and Michael, and even Nova pops up here and there. What was it about those characters that kept drawing you back in?

PAM: Sky is sort of a golden boy who's not really golden at all. I find those types of characters very interesting. Duplicitous characters. And I also like the idea of somebody who's the reluctant hero, somebody who automatically does something without thinking. There was a time when I saw my mom get in the middle of a fight in New York City, swinging her suitcase, while I stood back, panicking. She didn't even consider what she was doing, she just wanted to get between this big mean looking guy and a little skinny fellow who was getting the shit knocked out of him. I am in awe of the sort of person/character who moves forward without even thinking about it and who tries to help, and in some cases, tries to save people. When you put a character like that—a genuine do-gooder—in direct juxtaposition to a phony one, things can get interesting. Particularly for the people who surround them. Who believes in whom? Who can be trusted, who can be admired?

I also am intrigued by teenagers on the verge; I think that they're really rich characters. Their worldview isn't fully formed yet; they are willing to take things apart and try to make sense of situations they don't yet understand in a way adults don't always have time for. Sky and Michael don't grow very much from the place where they were when the book first started. Their paths were set in that first story, I think. So I thought about how these characters would be similar to who they were in SLF after some time had passed. It's interesting to me how characters like these guys and a place like New Hope can change so little over a number of years, and yet, even as things in the story don't shift all that much, a reader's perception can evolve.

Nova pops up again here and there, too. And while this book is finished, I don't think I'm entirely done with Nova. I think there are other stories I have to write about her eventually. I haven't yet figured out what they are, which is why I'm letting her take a break.

DP: With a town named New Hope, it seems like there should be so much possibility there, but there is a sense of everybody being stuck there.

PAM: When I first started writing some of these stories, New Hope was the name of the next town over, but I thought, "What if all these things happen in the town called New Hope?" That sense of some possibility contrasted with the idea of being stuck either by choice, or fear, or loyalty, or whatever it is that keeps people in a place is important to my understanding of what these stories are about. I think that "stuck-edness" happens a lot. I met an older woman in Mount Carroll who is probably in her 80s, maybe 90s. She told me that she has lived in Mount Carroll all her life, and I said, "Oh, you must really like it." And she said, "Like's got nothing to do with it. It's just where I'm from."

I always have a real wanderlust in me, and I couldn't imagine being someplace just because you're there. And so that started to become present in the stories, too. Some of these characters have come to New Hope as an escape, a need to be somewhere else, and yet they become stuck as well. A familiar place can be comfortable, sure, but you don't move too much and you end up with bedsores.

DP: It seems like a lot of the characters are hiding, in some ways.

PAM: "The Twin" was the very last story I wrote. Bert and Ernie were in the first piece I wrote, and I wondered, "What's their story?" It was interesting to go back and figure that out. Even though they came there hiding, literally on the run, they end up stuck, too.

The narrator in "The Things That'll Keep You Alive" is also

hiding somewhat. She has returned to the place she grew up, the home that was her parents, as a way to leave behind the unpleasantness her life in the city had become.

DP: Take me through the process of creating the collection, which finally became *Temple of Air*.

PAM: In the first draft of the collection, they were very loosely linked stories. But I thought that I really wanted to make it a novel in stories—who knows why, marketing? a personal challenge?—so I wrote all these "connective tissue" stories that have not survived because they were so obviously poor substitutes for real chapters. I finally figured out that I was more like trying NOT to write a novel than I was trying to write a solid novel-in-stories, so I decided I would be better served to collect a group of linked stories.

I reconsidered all of the stories I'd been writing, read them out loud, listened for the ones that seemed to have the legs to stand on their own independently of the rest of the collection. I teased those stories out, worked and reworked them. I took out the stories that didn't work very well on their own. I had submitted the original manuscript to a contest, and it made it into the top ten, but the judges said that its failure was that it tried too hard to be a novel-in-stories—which was absolutely true. When I extracted the fake story-chapters, the book became more solid.

It helped that along the way I was sending out the stories and getting a number of them published. All the stories in this collection have been published previously—except for one—in anthologies or journals. The ones that were connective tissue were not getting anywhere. So I started to pay attention to the wisdom of the audience beyond the front door.

And then, when I evaluated what was left and the way these stories sort of spoke to one another or overlapped, I started to think, "What if that girl was actually the waitress in this place?"

I didn't have to make a big deal of this, the small overlappings, the coincidences, like I was trying to do when I thought this was a novel-in-stories. I can just give the waitress the same name as that other character, and that would be it. It makes sense that this girl would grow up to be a waitress, or this boy would become a thief. Or—what else do we know about Sky? What if this guy were Sky along the way? What other things would he be up to?

DP: This constant inquiry must have required you to play with the narrative timeline.

PAM: The timeline is something I've played with a lot. I kept considering how many contemporary popular culture references did I want in the book. There was a lot of moving things about. I bet if I were to look at the collection again in three months, it might change. This is the way, I think, that it needs to go. I mean, I think that a collection of short stories has to have a certain sense of aliveness, of life going on before and after each of the stories start and finish, and this understanding can make each story shift even just a little bit if you don't just finally release them. Who was it that said "it's all a draft until we die?" A lot of the final rewriting has happened because another story has found its way in. Then I had to try to understand how that story affects this story immediately before, and how does it affect the story immediately after. How does it affect the whole story arc? I've spent a lot of time looking at the ripples made by each story as it goes in. Moving the elephant they say. Pick up the ear, the tail falls.

DP: Could you take us through your revision process for one of the stories?

PAM: I think that the story that went through the most rewriting and the most dramatic revisions would be "Running." I spent probably twelve to fifteen years of revision on that one.

The first draft of the story came from a dream. I know that I am not the only person who wakes up from a dream and thinks "Now that would make a great story." We are usually woefully wrong about this, by the way. I woke up the morning after the dream and started to write the story. I knew that there was something there but I couldn't make the story work because it was so true to the dream.

I was still a grad student at the time. I was invited to read it at the Printers' Row Book Fair in Chicago, by some fellow grad students (they'd heard a section of it in class, I think) and it was at the fair that I realized the story had a lot of dead air in it. It couldn't really rise above the noise of Printer's Row (an outside, busy, loud, literary event); the story didn't even want to rise above the noise. It didn't have the necessary dynamism, so I set it aside. And then I took it to a summer workshop, where I worked with a very strong female short story writer. She and the participants liked some things about the piece, they didn't like other things, but still, I couldn't find the real push behind the narrative. It didn't—I didn't—have an accurate read of what was really going on between the couple. So I reworked it and reworked it.

Reading out loud is always an important part of my process. I can get lost in the rhythms of a story, and "Running" has its own rhythm that I hear best when I read it out loud. So that was beginning to come through for me, but I, it, was still missing something.

Then in 2001, I had an opportunity to be writer-in-residence at Interlochen Arts Academy in Northern Michigan. I'm a regular runner, and I would run the same logging path every day while I was at Interlochen, and it was during these runs that the story started to present itself to me again. Some of the things that I talk about the character seeing on her run are things that I saw on my run: the clothes being sold and the crosses alongside country roads that look freshly painted even though they've been there for twenty years. I had a student at Interlochen who was writing a story about getting lost in the woods. We talked about that sense of freedom you get by being lost. Since you don't really know where you're going, it doesn't matter where you get to. That started to lift itself up and be more present in my story. I had already created the character of Arnold Huffner, and I thought, "How would that change this story if he were the man in the couple? What if he had asthma, for instance?"

DP: So you imagine specific character traits to create complications that drive the plot.

PAM: A story works best for me if there are a few different (at first) unobvious connections that begin to braid together, create metaphors and motifs. The idea that Hoof couldn't breathe, that he felt trapped, that Jackie felt trapped with him, that she couldn't comfort him in any way, that he pushes her away whenever she tries to comfort him, these all started to show themselves. In another story you find out that he feels she only loves him best when he needs comfort. There are these things that they're not understanding about each other, about their relationship.

I sent the story off to a couple places, and as happens more often than not, it got rejected. So I put it in a drawer. I lost faith in that story entirely. I thought, "I don't know how to fix this story. I've been working on it for nine years now." And then I had one of these really lucky breaks when a journal was interested in another story of mine that isn't part of this collection, but it was about twice as long as they wanted. They asked if I had anything else. I looked through other stories I had that fit their word count, and I found "Running," and I thought, "This isn't as bad as I remember it being." I did a little tweaking here and there and submitted it, and they published it. It gave me faith in the story again.

It was first-person when I wrote it, but I didn't want to have every story in first person in this collection. So I decided, right before we went to editing, that I'd give her a name; make her Jackie instead of "I." Part of it was a stylistic challenge on my part. I'm not particularly fond of present tense stories, but they're extremely prevalent in contemporary fiction. You see a lot of present tense in the first person, so I decided to try third-person present tense. It had a different sound, I think, than some of the other stories in the collection. I wanted to get a bit of a range, and even though the stories circle back to a lot of the same things, I wanted them to be told slightly differently. I kind of liked it in this third person present tense. It seemed to have more distance—despite what many people say about present tense, that it has more immediacy. Ultimately, Hoof is the character that I think the book has more of an allegiance to, so it didn't bother me that Jackie became more distant in this story. It shifts to past tense at the end. To me, the present tense held more possibility for her, and in the past tense, she gets stuck again in the end of the story. Present tense: this is how it could have gone; past tense: this is how it is/was.

DP: There are a couple of much shorter stories in *Temple of Air*. How does the process of writing them compare to writing longer pieces?

PAM: Most of my short pieces in fiction or nonfiction are what is salvageable from writing longer stuff. I think it's a big mistake to teach students to write short-shorts before you teach them to write long and seemingly unwieldy prose. In my opinion, you have to write long first. You have to figure out the bigness of things. I think you have to teach people how to push out for a while, and then trim back. I don't usually know what my stories are about for a really long time. I can go through twenty-five to thirty drafts of a story, and that can be anything from just changing names to totally restructuring.

I like the meandering possibilities of the longer story. My short-shorts very rarely start out as short-shorts. I don't think I've ever set out to write a short-short. I'll write something long, then find out there's only two pages that work. "The Joke" came out of a gazillion pages. In fact, it is the surviving part of my master's thesis, the only two pages. It's also the first story that I ever got published. As part of a much longer work, what became "The Joke" didn't have a sense of finality to it at first. I read it as it stood at a reading where readers had a one-page maximum. A. Manette Ansay was in the audience at that reading, and she told me afterward that it should be a short-short. It just needed to have a sense of conclusion to it. I had to figure out what it was about besides just what happens. The first draft of this piece was one of those things that pulled me out of bed in the middle of the night; I wrote it in a rush in my journal, getting it all down in an hour or so. But finishing it, finding its ending, took forever. Those final two lines went through maybe twenty-five drafts.

DP: How does real life inform your fiction?

PAM: I initially wrote "Deer Story" as creative nonfiction. I hit a deer when I was living in Iowa. I had this little Chevy Monza, and the collision totally sprung the body of my car. I was very young at the time, and I was living with a man I knew I was going have to leave. We had this house in a little subdivision outside of a small town. All of this became part of the story.

As I wrote it, I kept changing it from second person to first person and back again. Second person, particularly in creative nonfiction, can sometimes be a mask for first person, and yet when I settled on second person, I was able to move away from my own "real" experience and see the woman as a character. That helped me to realize that the character had participated in an indiscretion, and then it became a story instead of "I was driving home and hit a deer", just an anecdote. At the time I hit that deer for real, I did have a neighbor who'd shot his wife's face off, half of her face. All of this stuff was drawn very much from real life, but ultimately it is entirely fiction.

DP: How does teaching inform your writing and vice versa?

PAM: Probably most writing teachers will say what I have to say, which is that it's very hard to keep the writing going in its most effective way when you're teaching. Teaching makes me want very badly to write. I just finished the semester here and I can't wait to get to my own writing, not just as a way to be able to turn away from that every day responsibility of working on someone else's writing, but because, as in most semesters, I've encountered so many interesting ideas in the work of others. Looking at student work and watching them explore their own work always helps me to discover new things about my writing. I always learn new stuff when I read student work. But it's exhausting. You spend so much time reading student work and you come home and you want to just watch crappy TV because your eyes are hurting and your brain is hurting.

Our students, college students and grad students—if they are taking this writing thing seriously—are overwhelmed with work. They're trying to earn money; they're trying to have relationships; they probably are taking more credit hours than they should. But the committed ones are still getting the work—the writing—done. And so that, to me, is extremely inspiring. If they can do it, then I should be doing it. In some ways, because you have to steal time, you make that time count. I'm at a point with various projects that on those evenings when I'm not teaching, and those mornings that I don't have to be at Columbia too early, I'd rather turn back to the fiction than do just about anything else.

Writing and teaching can be like a good marriage. Half the time you're stepping on each other's toes, and the other half you're finishing each other's sentences. Half frustration, half total satisfaction. And because good marriages have about twelve halves, at least one other half is doing it just because.

Questions and Topics for Discussion

1. Though Sky, Nova, and Michael all witness the accident on the Gondolier, Sky ends up taking the credit for Michael's reaction. What is it in Sky's character that drives him to do this? What other examples of his behavior occur throughout the book?

2. In "Just Like That," we get a strong sense of the time in which the story occurs. Discuss the use of time in this story—the specter of the war in Vietnam—and throughout the book.

3. The town of New Hope lends a sense of gravity to the stories and becomes a character of its own. What do you think the significance of place is in the book? How does the place, setting, and landscape affect the characters and/or the events in the various stories?

4. In a few of the stories ("Running," "The Twin," "The Things That'll Keep You Alive") characters have relocated to New Hope from a larger city close by. What do they expect to find in their new homes? How do the urban characters differ from their rural neighbors? How are they similar? How does an outsider's point of view affect a reader's understanding of the situations and events of these stories?

5. "The Joke" is a deeply disturbing nugget of story. Discuss its brevity and what role these short-shorts ("The Joke," "Hand Thing," "Deer Story") play in the overarching narrative.

6. A number of the stories are told through the point of view of teen-aged narrators. How does the use of a teen-aged sensibility affect the way a story is told and what it is telling?

7. *The Temple of Air* spans decades in New Hope. What cues does McNair give the reader that time has shifted?

8. Cancer plays a central role in several stories. How does McNair handle cancer in different ways in "The Way it Really Went" and "The Things That'll Keep You Alive?" What does this say about the way gender affects the ability to cope?

9. Discuss how three main characters from the first story, "Something Like Faith"—Sky, Nova, and Mike—make it through the decades in New Hope. How do they act as markers for the narrative?

10. Henry and Robert ran from the city to New Hope. What role does guilt play in the stories of *The Temple of Air*?